AMELIA FANG
AND THE
MEMORY THIEF

AMELIA FANG

AND THE MEMORY THIEF

LAURA ELLEN ANDERSON

DELACORTE PRESS

For my marvelous, magnificent,
musical sister Marie!
The memories we've shared
are unforgettable and I love you
more than freshly baked cookies xxx

Text copyright © 2020 by Laura Ellen Anderson
Jacket art copyright © 2020 by Laura Ellen Anderson
Lettering and backgrounds copyright © 2020 by Sarah Coleman

All rights reserved. Published in the United States by Delacorte Press, an imprint of Random House Children's Books, a division of Penguin Random House LLC, New York.

Delacorte Press is a registered trademark and the colophon is a trademark of Penguin Random House LLC.

Visit us on the web! rhcbooks.com

Educators and librarians, for a variety of teaching tools, visit us at RHTeachersLibrarians.com

Library of Congress Cataloging-in-Publication Data is available upon request.
ISBN 978-0-593-17247-6 (trade)—ISBN 978-0-593-17248-3 (ebook)

The text of this book is set in 13-point Cosmiqua Com Light.

Printed in the United States of America

10 9 8 7 6 5 4 3 2 1
First American Edition

CONTENTS

FAIRY FOREST

THE MARVELOUS MOUNTAINS

THE KINGDOM OF THE LIGHT

RAINBOW RAIL STOP

PLEASANT POND

WISHING WELL OF WELL WISHES

THE BUG BLOSSOMS

FRUITFUL FRUIT TR

MEADOW OF LOVELINESS

THE PETRIFIED FOREST

FLORENCE'S PIT

AUNT MAVIS'S PIT

GOBLINS A

ZOMBIE YOGA HALL

CENTRAL NOCTURNIA GRAVEYARD

NOCTURNIA PALACE

THE CITY OF NOCTURNIA

THE PETRIFIED TREE-THAT-LOOKS-LIKE-A-UNICORN

THE HAUNTED HOUSES

RAINBOW RAI STOP

POST-BAT DEPOT

TOAD TOP HATS

THE IMP MOUN

THE PUMPKIN PATCH

TOAD BRIDGE

THE FANG MANSION

RIVER GLEE
DAZZLING DOCKS
GNOME NEIGHBORHOOD
TWINKLE TOWN
SPARKLE SPA
LEPRECHAUN LAGOON
RAINBOW RAIL STOP
FULL MOON MEADOWS
RAINBOW RAIL STOP
PUMPKIN PARADISE PARK
THE SCARY SUBURBS
BARGE
THE RICKETY RESIDENCES
ACADEMY
PUTRID POND
THE KINGDOM OF THE DARK
PITS
FALLS

Ghoulish Greetings!

AMELIA FANG
AND SQUASHY

LIKES:
Hanging out with friends
Pumpkin Paradise Park!

DISLIKES:
Mean creatures
Tidying up her bedroom

LIKES:
Scream-Cheese Boogers
Singing songs about life

DISLIKES:
Being confused
Rude zombies

TANGINE
AND PUMPY

LIKES:
Playing Goblin Tag
Throwing peas

DISLIKES:
Cooking class
Too much homework

FLORENCE AND GRIMALDI

COUNT DRAKE AND COUNTESS FRIVOLEETA

LIKES:
Playing Dungeons
and Daymares with
the king and queen

Wooo's Flabbergasting
Fettucine

DISLIKES:
Non-shiny toilets

LIKES:
Pushing wheelbarrows
Helping out

DISLIKES:
Not pushing wheelbarrows
Not helping out

KARL

HELEN

LIKES:
Not much

DISLIKES:
Most things

QUEEN FAIRYWEATHER

LIKES:
Playing Dungeons and
Daymares with the Fangs

Spending time with
Tangine

DISLIKES:
Megalomaniacs
Goblin slime in the library

AND KING VLADIMIR

CHAPTER 1

GOBLIN-SLIME SUPERGLUE

On a misty Wednesday night after school, young vampire Amelia Fang sat in her bedroom with her pet pumpkin, Squashy, surrounded by a complete and utter mess.

"Darkling," Amelia's mother, Countess Frivoleeta, called from downstairs. "It's time for your organ practice with Wooo. Remember, your exam is coming up soon."

"Do I have to practice tonight?" Amelia replied, her heart sinking at the thought of more organ practice—despite how ghoulishly enthusiastic Wooo, their ghost butler, was.

"I'm making Squashy a cute costume for my birthnight party!"

Squashy squeaked and spun on the spot delightedly.

"Isn't it exciting, Squashy! Soon I'll be eleven moon-years old!" Amelia beamed, flicking through her *Positively Pumpkin* magazine. "And we get to celebrate in style at the Pumpkin Patch! Golly ghouls, I do love pumpkins."

Amelia wanted to be a Pumpkinologist more than anything in the whole world when she grew up—she could imagine studying and caring for pumpkins like Squashy forever!

Amelia also loved making things, and she especially loved making things for Squashy. Tonight her bedroom floor was covered in black-and-orange material, goblin-slime superglue and various cobwebbing tools.

The bedroom door creaked open, revealing

Countess Frivoleeta's huge beehive hairdo. When she saw the mess in Amelia's room, she gasped.

"Amelia, my dreadful little wart-picker, I can't see your bedroom floor!"

"It's creative mess." Amelia grinned. "Look, I'm making some sunglasses for Squashy and some tiny bow ties."

The countess made a strange noise. "Amelia Fang! It's like you're living in a goblin cave. Wooo is waiting for you in the organ room, so tidy this mess up and then go downstairs for your practice."

Amelia felt her cheeks flush. "But, Mom, it's nearly my birthnight, and I have so much to catch up on in *Positively Pumpkin*! Can't I skip organ practice just this week?"

"Certainly not, darkling—you already missed last week because you were at pumpkin-patch digging. Organ practice is important—pumpkin magazines are *not*."

Amelia sighed. "Okay, Mom, I'll be down in a minute," she said as the countess left the room. Sometimes it felt like her mom just didn't understand.

"Don't worry, Squashy. We'll have your costume ready, even if I have to stay up all day to finish it."

Squashy pa-doinged in excitement but landed on the tube of goblin-slime superglue, and a giant purple glob spurted all over Amelia's dress.

"Oh, no! Be careful, Squashy!" Amelia shrieked, looking down at the slimy patch.

But the little pumpkin leapt forward and landed on Amelia's lap—right slap-bang in the pile of goblin slime.

"Uh-oh!" cried Amelia. "You just sat in the glue. . . ."

Squashy tried to **pa-doing** out of her lap, but he was stuck.

Amelia looked around her bedroom in search of some glitter—the only thing that could dissolve goblin slime—but she couldn't see any.

"We have to hurry, Squashy," Amelia urged. "Wooo is waiting for me, and you're stuck to my lap. . . . Argh!"

She tried her best to pull her dress off, but it was difficult with a pumpkin stuck to the front of it. Amelia found herself caught half in and half out of the dress. Squashy had begun to squeak in a panic and was swinging from side to side, trying to free himself.

"Whoa! Squashy, what are you doing?" Amelia asked, trying to wriggle out of the tangled garment. "Stop it! You're making me lose balance!"

But, determined to free himself, the little

pumpkin kept on swinging—making Amelia stumble around the room like a frenzied zombie.

"OUCH!" she cried as she stomped on a small box full of buttons and lost her footing.

CRASH!

Amelia and Squashy went tumbling into the pumpkin-themed creations, sending them flying across the room.

A few seconds later, her mom burst through the door.

"What the gravestones is going on?" she exclaimed, surveying the carnage.

"Um . . . I can explain—" Amelia started to say.

"And what's happened to your dress?" her mother said sternly.

Amelia looked down. There was a massive rip where Squashy had been swinging.

"It was an accident, Mom, honest!" Amelia

said, scrambling to her feet. "I was just about to leave, and the glue spilt out and Squashy got stuck and—"

"I have had enough, Amelia!" the countess said, holding up a hand. She picked up a copy of *Positively Pumpkin*. "You've always got your head stuck in this silly magazine! You've been neglecting your vampiress etiquette studies and organ practice for too long now."

"It's not a silly magazine!" Amelia cried, snatching it away from her mom.

"Do NOT use that tone with me," the countess replied. "One more outburst like that and I'm canceling your *Positively Pumpkin* subscription!"

"But, Mom, that's not fair! It was an accident, and you know how important

pumpkins and Squashy are to me!" Amelia said.

Countess Frivoleeta's left eyeball twitched. But she composed herself.

"Wooo is waiting," the countess said through gritted fangs. "Change your dress, and then you had better be downstairs in two minutes." She swiftly left the room.

Amelia sighed and slumped to the floor. "Oh, Squashy," she said sadly. "I don't think Mom knows me at all."

CHAPTER 2

MY LIFE . . . IN SONG

"So, are you excited about your birthnight party, Amelia?" said Grimaldi Reaperton the next night before school. "I heard your mom and dad rented the Pumpkin Patch for a whole night!"

Amelia sat quietly, tickling Squashy's tummy. "I guess so," she sighed.

Amelia and her best friends, Grimaldi, Florence Spudwick and Prince Tangine La Floofle the First sat under the Petrified-Tree-That-Looked-Like-a-Unicorn. Florence was a huge hairy yeti, an extremely loyal friend and a great pit-digger who did NOT like being called a beast by anybody. Tangine, on the other hand, was half vampire, half fairy and fully enjoyed a good face scrub.

"A Pumpkin Patch birthnight party sounds super fun!" Tangine said. "I know Pumpy will love it!"

Pumpy, Tangine's genetically modified pet pumpkin, tried to roll over but fell asleep halfway through the roll.

"Although I've recently discovered Pumpy suffers from Chronic-Upside-Down-Sleep-Syndrome . . . ," Tangine said, giving Pumpy a nudge so that he was upright once again.

The huge pumpkin flexed his six-pack

and PA-DOOFed into Tangine's arms, making the prince fall backward.

"*PRINCE DOWN!*" Florence yelled as Tangine groaned.

Amelia tried to smile but couldn't do it.

"You seem sad, Amelia," Grimaldi said. "What's up?"

"Me and Mom kind of had an argument," Amelia sighed. "I told her I didn't want to play the organ this week so that I could finish Squashy's costume—and read more *Positively Pumpkin*. And she got really mad. I just don't think I can be the perfect vampiress she wants me to be."

"THAT'S TOO BAD," Florence said, putting a big hairy arm around Amelia's shoulders. "YOU'LL BE HAPPY YOU STUCK WITH THE ORGAN, THOUGH. I WISH I COULD PLAY." She yawned.

Amelia and her friends were all feeling a little tired after the big Petrifying Palace Parade a few nights before, where everyone had celebrated the Kingdom of the Dark and the Kingdom of the Light becoming friends.

After many years of being completely terrified of each other, Creatures of the Light and the Dark could now live side by side in peace, since the evil Alpha Unicorn had been defeated by Amelia and her friends. Along with a group of mighty unicorn lords, Alpha Unicorn had been spreading false and scary rumors about the creatures from each kingdom to keep them divided. But thanks to Amelia and the gang, everyone was now free to roam wherever they pleased. Things were better than ever, and the Creatures of the Dark now accepted the wonders of glitter; once the stuff of nightmares!

The parade had been a LOT of fun, but

after much dancing, singing and pumpkin juggling, Amelia and her friends could have used more sleep.

From across the graveyard came the rattling sound of the Catacomb Academy welcome bones.

"C'MON, FANG," Florence said to Amelia. "I'M SURE A BIT OF BORING OLD SCHOOL WILL HELP CHEER YOU UP!"

Amelia couldn't help but chuckle. "Squashy, you can stay out here in the graveyard and play with Pumpy while we're at school." She gave the little pumpkin a pat on the stem.

Squashy pa-doinged once and blew a raspberry at Pumpy. Pumpy responded by puffing his six-pack chest out at Squashy.

"You two need to learn to be friends," Amelia said kindly. "I hope you are by the time school finishes."

Amelia would usually sneak Squashy into

class with her, but she felt having a pumpkin buddy would be good for him. It didn't stop her from missing Squashy every second they were apart, though. Luckily, Amelia had lots of new school subjects to focus on and keep her mind occupied.

Since the Kingdom of the Dark and the Kingdom of the Light had become friends, Catacomb Academy had introduced a variety of new Kingdom of the Light–themed lessons to educate the Creatures of the Dark. Alongside Pumpkinology and Slime Skills, Amelia and her friends now studied Angel-

Kitten Singing, Cloud Crafts, Glitterology and History of the Bug Blossoms.

"Good evening, class," said the teacher, Miss Inspine, as the students settled onto their plinths. "Firstly, I'd like to welcome the fairy exchange students from the Kingdom of the Light. I appreciate you may be a little sleepy while you get used to the time difference," said Miss Inspine, addressing the fairies.

Five fairies, who were all different sizes, waved shyly from the back of the classroom, not looking at all alarmed that their new teacher was a skeleton. One teeny-weeny fairy with a puffy dress had fallen asleep inside a test tube and was snoring loudly.

"Now, class, you may remember I asked you all to put together a presentation on a subject of your choice, to introduce our visitors to the Kingdom of the Dark," Miss Inspine continued. "Tangine, I believe you're up first— what is the title of your presentation?"

Tangine stood and strutted to the front of the classroom.

"May I present to you, MY LIFE... IN SONG," Tangine said, straightening his bow tie.

Amelia, Florence and

Grimaldi looked at each other wide-eyed, trying not to laugh.

"Um . . . ," began Miss Inspine. But before she could continue, Tangine bellowed:

"CLASSMATES, AND FAIRIES FROM AFAR!"

"Oh, he's actually doing this . . . ," Amelia whispered, a little surprised. She'd never heard Tangine attempt to sing before.

"Thiiiiiis story of sadness, this tale of delight . . .
Is one of the Creatures of Dark and of Liiiiiight.
For both lived in fear of the other for years,
Led by stories of beasts—"

"I AM NOT A BEAST!" Florence blurted out, causing the snoring fairy in the test tube to wake with a start.

Tangine glared.

"UH, SORRY . . . NEVER MIND," Florence said sheepishly.

Clearing his throat, Tangine continued theatrically.

"Led by stories of beasts and unicorn tears!
Two Kingdoms divided by terror and lies,
But soon they'd be in for a pleasant surpriiiiise!
One twilight, the King of Nocturnia met
A fairy?!
Oh dear!
But she was not a threat. . . .
She was kind, a true beauty, the love of his life,
And this fairy became King Vladimir's wiiiiiife!"

"Wow," Amelia whispered to her friends. "He's actually really good!"

"And soon baby Tangine was born. . . .

Yes, that's MEEEEE!
The *most* handsome baby you ever did see.
With the fangs of a vampire and fairy wings too?!
Nobody could find out—who knows what they'd do?

Then suddenly, one dusk, my mother was gone.
The king wondered if he'd done something
wrong.
He searched every night, every day, *all* year through,
And the older I got, the more distant he
grew. . . ."

Tangine then got down on one knee and cast
his hand across his forehead dramatically.

"I was spoiled, I was lonely, and then I started school.
But I acted a bit like a silly young fool!
I stole a pet pumpkin and took someone's chair,
But a special friend showed me how that
wasn't fair."

Tangine looked at Amelia and blushed.

Amelia beamed back, happy that she and Tangine were now such good friends.

"She found out my secret, but *she* wasn't scared,
And that's how I knew that my friend really cared.
We went on a journey to find my lost mom,
To the Kingdom of the Light in the dazzling sun!

But little did we know that the unicorn lords—
Those mighty horned horses their citizens adored—
Had kidnapped my mother! Oh yes, you heard right!
So we grabbed our baguettes and we put up a fight!"

"HEH HEH." Florence chuckled at the memory of brandishing bread baguettes and baked goods as weapons against Alpha Unicorn and his unicorn lords.

"The truth was revealed—and my mother
was freeeeeeed!
Creatures of the Light and the Dark all agreed,
We've no need to fear one another anymore.
Together we've so much to learn and explore!
So the King of Nocturnia is now full of glee!
(Even though he was briefly turned into a bee.
Yes, really.)
And that's the tale of how two
kingdoms made amends,
And how the Creatures of the Light and the
Dark became frieeeeeeeeends!"

Tangine threw both arms in the air and sent
glitter flying across the classroom. Once upon
a time this would have terrified his Creature
of the Dark classmates, but now everyone
cheered and clapped and twirled around in
the glittery rainstorm.

Amelia stood up, chanting Tangine's name, followed by Grimaldi and then Florence. The fairies appeared to be crying sparkly tears of joy.

"Tangine La Floofle," Miss Inspine said with a look of shock on her skull. "That was quite possibly the best presentation any student has ever given in my class. WELL DONE!"

CHAPTER 3

SUBLIME

After lunch, Amelia and her friends made their way to the Coughing Classroom, in the most-hidden halls of Catacomb Academy, for a brand-new lesson.

"I WONDER WHAT OUR NEW LESSON IS," said Florence.

"I hope it's more fun than Zombie Social Studies," Grimaldi said.

Amelia giggled. "I'm excited to meet our new teacher," she said. "I heard it might be someone from Glitteropolis!"

Amelia and her friends approached the classroom, where a plump and wrinkly man with thick-rimmed glasses, a big curly

mustache and *huge* fairy wings was waiting by the door.

"STUDENTS!" He smiled, his teeth shining blindingly white. "Come in, come in! Welcome, welcome!"

Amelia, Florence, Grimaldi and Tangine took seats at the back of the classroom, carefully avoiding any snot that the Coughing Classroom spluttered in their direction.

As Amelia looked around the Coughing Classroom, she noticed it had been decorated from top to bottom with glossy printouts of Ravishing Recipes and pictures of the new teacher posing with various cooking implements.

Once the class had settled down, the teacher half skipped to the front of the classroom and threw his arms out as if he were about to invite everyone over for a great big hug.

"Hellooooo, students of Catacomb Academy!" he sang. "I am *terribly* delighted to be joining you all in your wonderfully dark and gloomy city of Nocturnia. I'm your new culinary teacher, Mr. Sublime!"

"Oooh, culinary class!" said Amelia and Tangine in unison.

"HEH, SOUNDS LIKE MR. SLIME," Florence huffed.

"Florence!" Amelia whispered, half-smiling.

"I can't wait to share some of

my favorite Glitteropolan recipes with you. We're going to have a *lot* of fun making a LOT of food!" Mr. Sublime said.

Tangine's eyes lit up and a string of dribble slipped its way down his chin. "Hmmmm, *fooooood!*" he gurgled happily.

AHEM!

"Yes?" said the teacher, looking around at the students expectantly for more signs of appreciation.

"IT WASN'T ANY OF US THAT MADE

THAT NOISE, MR. SLIME. THAT WAS THE ROOM. THAT'S WHY IT'S CALLED THE COUGHING CLASSROOM," Florence explained.

"Oh, I see," Mr. Sublime said, looking a little ill as he watched a trickle of snot slide down the back wall, between two particularly dramatically posed pictures of himself with a frying pan.

Grimaldi was trying not to laugh.

Amelia elbowed Florence in the belly. "You can't call him Mr. Slime!" she whispered. "It's Mr. *Sublime*!"

Grimaldi and Florence smirked.

Recovering himself, the teacher flung his arms out wide. "Well, let's get started with your first culinary class like no other! And do you know WHY it's like no other?" Mr. Sublime didn't wait for anyone to answer. "Because it has been said by *many*—not myself, you understand—that *I* am the BEST cook you've ever met or are likely to meet."

"How is he so sure?" whispered Grimaldi. "I always thought my grimpapa was the best cook around. . . ."

"I think you'll find Wooo is *definitely* the best!" Amelia replied.

"Tonight, class, we will be making my favorite recipe!" continued Mr. Sublime.

"I wonder if it's *Boasting Buns*!" Grimaldi giggled.

"*Oh,* no . . . we'll be making *those* next week," said the teacher, looking straight at Grimaldi, whose deathly pale cheeks flushed with embarrassment. "This week, we'll be making Sublime Cookies!"

"HEH, SLIME," Florence said.

Tangine rolled his eyes. "Are you going to do that *every* time?"

"YEAH, AND WHAT'S IT TO YOU?" Florence said, nudging Tangine off his plinth.

"You'll find a copy of my recipe book *It's SUBLIME Time!* on your desks. Find a partner and turn to page fifty-five for the Sublime Cookie recipe," the teacher started. "All the ingredients you need are on the table at the back of the classroom."

Spoons and spatulas clinked and clunked as the class split off into pairs and began making cookies. Amelia paired with Tangine, who had grabbed five whisks to mix with. Florence and Grimaldi teamed up and seemed more interested in flicking ingredients into Grimaldi's eye socket than making the cookies.

"Stop messing around, you two," said Amelia as a Perfumed Pea went flying into her mixing bowl. "You'll get us into trouble before we've even finished our first lesson! Also, what *are* you doing with those peas? There *aren't* any Perfumed Peas in this recipe."

"SORRY," said Florence, getting ready to shove another Perfumed Pea up Grimaldi's nose. "COOKING'S NOT REALLY MY THING. . . ."

"What?" said Tangine, raising his eyebrows. "Cooking is *so* fun!"

"THE EATING
PART IS FUN. JUST
NOT THE MAKING PART,"
Florence said.

"Well, keep your peas to yourself." Amelia smiled. "Tangine and I actually *want* to cook!"

As Amelia studied the Sublime Cookie recipe, she couldn't help giggling at the pictures of Mr. Sublime in a flowery apron.

"First, we need to combine one hundred and fifty grams of Sunflower Root with two spatulas of powdered Scorpion Grass . . . ," Amelia said, reading through a list of ingredients. "Wow, I've never heard of any of these things before."

"That's because they can only be found in the Fairy Forest in the Kingdom of the Light," said a voice next to Amelia, making her jump.

"Oh!" she exclaimed. "Hello, Mr. Sublime . . ."

Florence leaned over. "HEH, SLI—"

"Don't!" interrupted Tangine, shoving a spatula in Florence's mouth.

Grimaldi now had around fifty Perfumed Peas in his eye socket.

"The Fairy Forest is bursting with *millions* of amazing and mysterious plants. Even I, an expert, couldn't possibly know about them *all*!" Mr. Sublime said with a smile. "What's your name, young vampire?"

"Amelia Fang."

Mr. Sublime raised his eyebrows. "I believe I've heard of you."

"And I'm Prince Tangine!" added Tangine. "You've probably *most definitely* heard of *me*, because I'm sort of famous."

"You're the daughter of the Count and Countess Fang?" said Mr. Sublime, ignoring Tangine.

"Oh, yes," said Amelia shyly. "That's Mom and Dad." Her chest tightened as she remembered the argument she'd had with her mom the night before.

"I heard your mother puts on a ravishing Barbaric Ball every year!" Mr. Sublime exclaimed. "I expect you'll follow in her frightful footsteps?"

"Hmmm, she'd love that, but I'm not really into party planning and all that stuff," said Amelia, feeling a little deflated. "I really want to be a Pumpkinologist when I grow up."

Mr. Sublime leaned forward and lowered his voice. "Well, Amelia Fang, that's just *wonderful*. You remember to follow that cold vampiric heart of yours. You have a dream—don't let *anyone* get in the way of that!"

Amelia felt herself smiling from ear to ear. Mr. Sublime believed in her!

"I have dreams too! You can expect HUGE things from me!" Tangine said, throwing his arms up in the air.

"Amelia and, er, Prince . . . Tangy, I believe you both have a *sublime* future ahead of you, and don't you *forget* that," he added before wandering over to Florence and Grimaldi.

"OH, HI, MR. SLIME!" Florence bellowed. Grimaldi snorted with laughter so hard that the fifty Perfumed Peas flew out of his nostrils and into Amelia and Tangine's mixing bowl.

"You've ruined our Sublime Cookie mix!" Amelia groaned.

"SORRY ABOUT THAT," Florence said. "MAY YOUR COOKIES REST IN PEAS. . . ."

CHAPTER 4

PUMPKIN PARADISE PARK

By the end of the culinary lesson, Amelia and Tangine had made four batches of cookies, while Florence and Grimaldi had just made a mess.

"I hope you've all enjoyed your first cooking class with me!" Mr. Sublime beamed as Florence poked another ingredient into Grimaldi's eye socket. "I have one last exciting announcement . . . I am holding a special competition!"

The students murmured with anticipation at the word "competition."

"A SUBLIME Cookie Competition!" the

teacher enthusiastically told the classroom.

"I HAD A FEELING IT WOULD BE CALLED SOMETHING LIKE THAT," Florence said.

Tangine threw a Sunflower Root at Florence, hitting her between the eyes.

"All you have to do is make your *own* version of my Sublime Cookies and sell them to your family and friends," Mr. Sublime said. "The team who sells the most cookies will win a special trip to Pumpkin Paradise Park!"

Florence lowered the bowl of slime she was about to throw over Tangine. "OOO, I'VE HEARD THAT PLACE IS FUN!" she said.

"I've heard it's the BEST!" Amelia whispered. "I've *always* wanted to go!"

Amelia reached out and squeezed Tangine's hand in excitement. She'd read all about Pumpkin Paradise Park in her *Positively Pumpkin* magazine. It was one of the most exciting places in the kingdom, with pumpkin-themed rides, horror hotels, slime pools and the biggest pumpkin patch in all the Kingdom of the Dark.

"Just so you know, Amelia Fang, *I'm* going to win this competition," said a voice behind her. It was Frankie Steinburg—a total teacher's pet and the most annoying of Amelia's classmates.

Amelia gritted her fangs. "Humph. Well, we'll see about that."

Amelia knew she HAD to win the trip to Pumpkin Paradise Park. It would be a dream come true. But Frankie would be stiff competition.

The air was thick with the smell of rivalry.

"You'll need to split into teams of four . . . ," Mr. Sublime continued.

Amelia and Tangine exchanged a look, then

turned to Florence and Grimaldi, who were still messy. "Do you want to be a team of four?" Amelia asked a little hesitantly. "It means you'll have to do actual baking. Not just throwing the ingredients around . . ."

Grimaldi nodded sheepishly, and Florence grinned. "WE CAN CHANT ENCOURAGING WORDS WHILE YOU AND TANGINE BAKE."

Amelia sighed. She really hoped Florence wouldn't ruin their chances of winning the competition.

"Everybody!" Mr. Sublime sang over the commotion. He paused dramatically and pushed his glasses back up his nose. "You have ONE week to bake and sell as many cookies as possible."

Amelia felt her heart flutter at the thrill of it all.

"Don't forget to take your recipe books with you on your way out. All the basic ingredients to make Sublime Cookies are in there, but feel free to add a few of your own. Be inventive and make the BEST cookies possible! The tastier they are, the *more* you'll sell. Also—"

Before Mr. Sublime had even finished speaking, the students scrambled over each other to the back of the room, grabbing sacks of Scorpion Grass and Sunflower Root, tubes of Fairy Tears and tubs of Rose Petals.

ACHOOOO!

Snot sprayed toward the students at the ingredients table, stopping them in their path.

"Er, thank you, Classroom," Mr. Sublime said, wiping down his wings.

"As I was saying . . . I have made a special batch of Sublime Cookies with extra Scorpion Grass for you all to take home on your way out. Consider it a special treat to celebrate our first class together. And *look* . . . I decorated each one to look like *me*!"

Even Amelia couldn't help chuckling as she picked up a cookie iced with Mr. Sublime's face.

"I'll see you all again next week, and we can see who has sold the most cookies," Mr. Sublime said, putting his hands on his hips. "Good luck, everyone. And *don't forget* to have fun!"

CHAPTER 5

I JUST WANNA PLAY GOBLIN TAG

Squashy **pa-doing**ed straight into Amelia's arms when he saw her at the school entrance.

"Hey, Squashy!" Amelia said, squeezing him tight. "Did you and Pumpy have a good night?"

Squashy frowned in Pumpy's direction.

Pumpy **PA-DOOF**ed and spat out a pip-ball, along with some unchewed Honey-Roasted Maggots.

"Pumpy! You ate Squashy's lunch! Those maggots weren't for you," Amelia cried. "Tangine, you really need to teach him not to eat, well, *everything*. . . ."

"I'm trying," Tangine said. "He does it

without me even seeing. . . . Wait, where did my Sublime Cookie go?" He looked down to see Pumpy munching the last of Mr. Sublime's icing face, then burp.

"THIS SLIME COOKIE IS PRETTY TASTY," Florence said. "I PARTICULARLY ENJOYED EATING HIS CANDY NOSE."

Amelia grinned. "I guess we should get cracking with *our* cookie-making now."

"DO WE HAVE TO DO IT NOW?" Florence

asked. "CAN'T WE GO PLAY GOBLIN TAG?"

"I think we should get started as soon as possible if we want to stand a chance of winning the competition," Amelia said.

"BUT BAKING IS BORING," Florence grumbled. "MAYBE YOU AND TANGINE COULD DO THE BAKING PART. THEN ME AND GRIMALDI CAN CHEER YOU ON, OR DO THE TASTE TESTING?"

"C'mon, Florence! We *all* need to help out

with the cookie baking, so we can sell LOADS and *win*!" Amelia urged. "Then we get to go to the BEST theme park around!"

Florence harrumphed.

"I guess we could help bake a little," Grimaldi said, clearly feeling guilty. "We could measure stuff out?"

"I JUST WANNA PLAY GOBLIN TAG," Florence whined.

"And we *will*!" Amelia said. "As soon as we've baked some cookies. *Pleeeease*, Florence!"

Florence sighed. "FINE. ONLY 'CAUSE YOU LOOK LIKE YOU MIGHT EXPLODE IF I DON'T . . . AND I CAN'T PROMISE I WON'T THROW STUFF."

Amelia smiled with relief. They definitely wouldn't be able to win unless all four of them worked as a team.

"We can use the palace kitchen to bake if you like," Tangine suggested, digging in to a whole bag of Scream-Cheese Boogers.

"That's a great idea! Thanks, Tangine," Amelia said, taking a bite of her Sublime Cookie. "OUCH!"

Squashy squealed in reaction to Amelia crying out.

"Are you okay, Amelia?" Grimaldi asked, floating over to her.

Amelia spat out her mouthful of Sublime Cookie.

Pumpy PA-DOOFed over and lapped it up in one gulp.

"My fang really hurt when I took a bite," Amelia said, rubbing her cheek.

"Oh dear," said Grimaldi. "Sounds like a visit to the Crow Dentist for you!"

Amelia grimaced. She hated going to the dentist.

"IT'S A SIGN!" said Florence. "NO BAKING TONIGHT!"

Amelia frowned. "Not for me," she said sadly. "But that doesn't mean you three can't get started. I'll meet you all at Nocturnia Palace later, after I've seen the dentist. We'll bake loads of cookies and then we've got the weekend to sell them."

"I'll make sure the Mummy Maids clear the kitchen for us. We'll see you at the palace later, Amelia," said Tangine, before calling, "JOHN!"

A three-eyed vulture swept to the ground, squishing a small toad in the process and causing Grimaldi's diePhone (which alerted him to all unfortunate fatal toad mishaps) to start buzzing. Grimaldi had been dealing with more toad deaths than usual lately, due to John's clumsiness.

Tangine, Florence and Grimaldi took to the skies on the back of the pained-looking vulture.

"GOOD LUCK AT THE CROW DENTIST, AMELIA!" Florence called.

"Thanks, Florence," Amelia called back, waving. Then she headed home into the low mists of Nocturnia with a heavy heart and a very sore tooth.

CHAPTER 6

BAKE FASTER

Friday night after school, Amelia, Tangine, Florence and Grimaldi got ready to sell their Sublime Cookies to the Creatures of the Dark. Squashy and Pumpy were busy sniffing the cookie boxes, eager to get a look in.

"I'm so *so* sorry I couldn't join you to bake our cookies last night," explained Amelia. "I had to wait *forever* at the Crow Dentist, and Mom was still cross with me about my ruined dress, so she wouldn't let me come out. Sorry to let you down. But it looks like you made lots of cookies."

"Well *I* did," Tangine said. Amelia noticed he was an unusual shade of green tonight. *He must have borrowed his mom's royal face cream again,* she thought.

"Florence and Grimaldi were no help at all," Tangine added. "They just made a mess and threw the dough all over the floor. I even had to stop Florence from lying down and making food-angels in it. It was a daymare! Luckily, Karl, my Mummy Maid, helped me. Otherwise we'd have nothing to sell today."

Amelia looked crossly at Florence and Grimaldi.

"WHAT?" said Florence. "I TOLD YOU THERE WAS A STRONG POSSIBILITY I'D THROW STUFF."

"We did chant a nice song to cheer Tangine on while he baked, though," said Grimaldi, not looking Amelia in the eye.

"Incorrect," said Tangine flatly. "Florence mostly shouted 'BAKE FASTER' at me and called me COOKIE-FACE."

"WELL, IT CLEARLY WORKED!" Florence yelled, punching Tangine in the shoulder. "LOOK—YOU BAKED TEN BATCHES AND THEY TASTE AWESOME. YOU SHOULD TRY ONE, AMELIA!"

Amelia shook her head. "I'm not allowed. Strict Crow Dentist orders until my fang gets better," she said, rubbing her cheek.

"TOO BAD. MORE COOKIES FOR ME, THEN," said Florence, peering inside one of the boxes. "OOOH!" She grabbed a cookie and swallowed it whole. "THAT ONE WAS BELLY-BUTTON-FLUFF FLAVOR!"

"Hey! Florence, we're supposed to be selling them, not *eating* them all!" said Amelia, poking her friend's arm.

"RELAX. WE HAVE LOADS. MUNCHING ONE WON'T HURT. OR MAYBE TWO . . . ," said Florence, reaching to grab another. Amelia smacked her paw away.

"Yeah, Florence, you're not supposed to eat them," Grimaldi said, pointing his scythe at her. At the same time, a cookie fell out of his hood.

"BUSTED!" Florence shouted.

"Please," Amelia said. "Stop eating our supplies! We'll have nothing left to sell. Isn't that right, Tangine?"

Tangine didn't say anything.

"OI, TAN-GREEN!" Florence said, poking his cheek. "YOU'VE CHANGED COLOR. WHAT'S GOING ON WITH YOU?"

"I'm not feeling so good. I think I ate too many Scream-Cheese Boogers after school

last night," Tangine said, holding his tummy. "I'll be fine. Come on, let's sell these cookies!"

"YEAH. THE FASTER WE SELL 'EM, THE FASTER WE CAN GO PLAY GOBLIN TAG! IT IS A FRIDAY NIGHT, AFTER ALL!" Florence sang.

Amelia and her friends began their cookie quest around the city. As they weaved in and out of the streets of Nocturnia, Amelia noticed that the air smelled of flowers. As she breathed it in, looking up at the sky, she spotted some little blue specks drifting past her face and dancing through the night air.

"Where did those come from?" she asked curiously. Squashy bounced as high as he could, trying to catch one of the blue specks in his mouth.

"HOW WEIRD . . . ," Florence said, looking up.

"Never seen weather like this before," said Tangine, raising an eyebrow.

"If that's not a sign of Global Cooling, I don't know what is!" Grimaldi said, folding his arms.

"I'm not sure it's the weather," said Amelia as the friends approached the cave entrance to Goblins Anonymous. "It's like something is being blown along by the wind."

Forgetting all about the strange flecks, Amelia pulled on a long branch at the entrance of the huge Goblins Anonymous cave, and a high-pitched screeching sound announced their arrival.

"Oh, hello there," said a fat goblin with no teeth. "Are you here for the Worldly Wart Talk?"

"NAH," said Florence. "WE WERE WONDERING IF WE COULD INTEREST YOU AND YOUR FELLOW GOBLINS IN SOME COOKIES. YOU GOT A CHOICE OF THREE FLAVORS: RASPBERRY AND FRIGHT CHOCOLATE, SWEAT SYRUP SURPRISE, AND BELLY-BUTTON FLUFF."

"Oh, we already bought five boxes of Slug Slime Sublime Cookies from that lovely monster girl Frankie," said the goblin. "She gave us some free unicorn stickers too!"

Amelia clenched her fists in frustration. She couldn't believe Frankie Steinberg had got there before them.

Tangine stepped forward. "If you buy SIX boxes of OUR cookies, I'll take you on a private tour of Nocturnia Palace! You could sit on my dad's throne too. AND ride my three-eyed vulture!"

Pumpy nudged Tangine's leg, almost knocking him over.

"Oh, and you get to pat my pet pumpkin, Pumpy." Pumpy puffed out his chest to reveal his six-pack.

The goblin sighed. "If you'd been here fifteen minutes earlier, I'd have said yes, but we spent our weekly allowance on Frankie's cookies already. I'm terribly sorry. The stickers really swayed our decision!"

Feeling deflated, the friends moved on. They knocked on a small gravestone in Central Nocturnia Graveyard.

"Yes?" came a voice from underground.

"WE HAVE COOKIES, AND YOU'RE GONNA HURRY UP AND BUY THEM SO I CAN GO PLAY!" said Florence.

A zombie hand burst out of the ground, brandishing a cookie. "Got some Armpit-Flavored Sublime Cookies already from that Frankie girl. She gave us a ton of free Cheese and Bunion Crisps too. What you got to offer? We could do with some Whole-Brain Bread."

"No Whole-Brain Bread, but how about half a pack of Nefarious Nuts?" Tangine asked, searching his pockets.

"Not interested. Now move on, I'm trying to sleep here!" the zombie said.

"Rude!" Tangine said, making sure to stomp extra hard as he passed over the zombie's grave.

Next, the friends visited the Rickety Residences, where some of the biggest stars in Nocturnia lived, including the Howling Wolf Band.

"Ah, sorry, mate," said Gibbous, the band's drummer. "We got forty-two boxes of the Beetle Brain flavor from someone called Frankie. We need to watch the ol' sugar levels."

"THIS IS TURNING INTO A MASSIVE WASTE OF TIME," said Florence. "MIGHT AS WELL EAT THE COOKIES OURSELVES."

"We have to keep trying," Amelia said. "We still haven't tried the Yeti Mountain Pits, or the Post-Bat Depot . . . or the Scary Suburbs!"

"I'M TIRED OF SELLING COOKIES," said Florence. "CAN'T WE TRY AGAIN TOMORROW?"

"But we won't win if we don't hurry," Amelia urged. "We have to beat Frankie! And remember, we get a trip to Pumpkin Paradise Park if we win!"

"I KNOW, BUT I'M BORED!" huffed Florence. "I'M GONNA GO PLAY GOBLIN TAG. ARE YOU ALL COMING?"

Amelia shook her head. She wasn't in a very playful mood.

Tangine stayed unusually quiet.

"FINE. C'MON, GRIMALDI. LET'S GO."

Grimaldi looked awkwardly from Amelia to Florence. "I . . . I . . . Um . . ."

"Fine," Amelia said grumpily as Florence dragged a tongue-tied Grimaldi away. "But it would be nice if you could be a bit more helpful tomorrow, Florence."

Florence grunted and kept walking. Tangine didn't seem to be saying much at all.

"See you by the Petrified-Tree-That-Looks-Like-a-Unicorn at moonrise to continue, then!" Amelia called after her friends.

"FINE," Florence grumbled.

"Don't be late!" Amelia yelled after her. She turned to Tangine. "You'll be there, right?"

But instead of replying, Tangine threw up.

CHAPTER 7

BAD BOOGERS

At moonrise on Saturday night, Amelia waited for her friends under the Petrified-Tree-That-Looked-Like-a-Unicorn.

"Where is everyone, Squashy?" asked Amelia, rubbing his tummy. "It's not like them to be so late. I hope Florence isn't still mad at me. I feel bad for being so grumpy toward her."

An hour went by, but still there was no sign of Florence, Grimaldi or Tangine. Fed up with waiting, Amelia decided that if they weren't coming to her, she would go to them. She headed off to Nocturnia Palace to find Tangine.

Amelia knocked on the huge golden door.

"Hello, is Tangine there?" she asked when an unraveled Mummy Maid in a pink towel appeared.

"The prince is sick," said the Mummy Maid.

"Oh," Amelia said. "I hope he's okay."

"Well, no, because he's *sick*," said the Mummy Maid. Pumpy PA-DOOFed into view, then rolled over and fell asleep. Tangine hobbled to the door, looking a very unpleasant shade of green.

"It's okay, Helen." Tangine waved a hand at the agitated Mummy Maid. "Go and finish your foot-spa session. Hey, Amelia." He winced and held his tummy.

"Oh, no," said Amelia. "I'm sorry you're ill."

"I think there was something off with the boogers I ate. I've been sick all day. It's all green and lumpy too."

Amelia grimaced. "I really didn't need to know that."

"I don't think I can face selling cookies right now." Tangine puffed his cheeks out and made a weird noise.

"Don't worry, Tangine," Amelia said, taking a step back. "You should stay in bed and get better. Florence, Grimaldi and I will deal with the cookie selling tonight."

"Where are they?" Tangine asked, peering behind Amelia.

"I have no idea. Nobody came to meet me,"

said Amelia. "I'm worried they're still angry with me."

"I'm sure they're fine. Florence isn't the type to stay angry. She just doesn't like missing an opportunity to play Goblin Tag." Tangine said, giving a strained smile.

"True," said Amelia. "Well, I'd better go and find her. Hopefully you'll be better for my birthnight party tomorrow!"

"I'll be there no matter what!" said Tangine punching the air weakly. "That's what friends d—" But he didn't finish his sentence because he ran off to be sick again.

Amelia decided it was probably time to go.

She wandered through Central Nocturnia Graveyard toward Florence's pit in the Petrified Forest, keeping an eye out for her friends. Squashy bounced beside her happily. Where the bats *were* they? Amelia wondered.

She finally spotted Florence by the edge of the River Styx doing one-armed push-ups, with a plate of cookies next to her.

"HEY, AMELIA!" Florence called. Every time she did a push-up, she grabbed a cookie between her teeth and gobbled it whole.

"Florence! How come you didn't meet me earlier? You're not still mad about yesternight, are you?" Amelia asked.

"MEET YOU? WHERE? MAD? HUH?" Florence seized another cookie with her tongue.

"You and your jokes, Florence." Amelia laughed uncertainly.

"I DUNNO WHAT YOU'RE TALKING ABOUT." Florence looked at her blankly. "COOKIE?"

Amelia frowned and picked Squashy up for

comfort. He licked at her cheek as she mumbled, "I can't have any cookies."

"BUT THEY'RE SUBLIME!" Florence laughed. "GO ON, TRY ONE." She picked at her teeth with a claw.

"You *know* I can't . . . ," Amelia started. "I have a sore fang."

"OH, TOO BAD," Florence said, and kept on munching. "SO," she continued through a mouthful of cookie. "WHAT ARE WE GONNA DO NOW? I WAS THINKING GOBLIN TAG!"

"Enough with the goblin tag, Florence! We're *supposed* to be selling our cookies to win the competition—not *eating* them all!" Amelia was growing impatient.

Florence looked confused.

"I DON'T KNOW NOTHIN' ABOUT NO COMPETITION!" she said.

Amelia stood in silence for a few seconds. "Stop being silly, Florence. Look. I'm sorry about yesternight, but I've got a good feeling we'll sell lots of cookies tonight!"

"SERIOUSLY. WHAT *ARE* YOU TALKING

ABOUT?" Florence asked. "STOP BEING WEIRD."

"*You're* the one being weird!" Amelia snapped. She sighed. "I think I'm just going to go home."

"WHY'S THAT?" said Florence. "WE'VE GOT THE WHOLE NIGHT AHEAD OF US! YOU OKAY?"

Amelia shuffled on the spot. "Actually, I'm suddenly not feeling well." Amelia felt a flutter of guilt, as this wasn't entirely true, but she wasn't feeling great, either.

"ALL RIGHT," Florence said. "FEEL BETTER SOON! I'LL SAVE YOU A COOKIE!"

Amelia ran as fast as she could back to the Fang Mansion, with Squashy held tightly in her arms. As she hurried through the front door, she almost walked through Wooo.

"Young Amelia. You look all droopy and

sad. Whatever is wrong?" the ghost butler asked kindly.

"Florence and Grimaldi forgot to meet me to sell cookies tonight. We're supposed to be working together to win the school competition," said Amelia. "And poor Tangine is sick, so he can't help right now either."

"Don't be sad," said Wooo. "I'm sure everything will work out fine. But speaking of your little death friend, Grimaldi—there's a rather large pile of squished toads in the

back garden. Some vulture landed on them. They've been there for hours, and your mother is worried they're making the place look untidy."

"How odd. It's not like Grimaldi to leave a toad pile-up untouched," said Amelia. She wondered if she should go and find him, but Florence had acted so strange, Amelia wasn't sure she wanted to see anyone else right now.

She hugged Squashy to her chest. He always made her feel better.

"Oh, Wooo," said Amelia. "I've had such a horrible couple of nights. Mom is angry with me because I ruined my dress—she says that I think about pumpkins too much. And I'm pretty sure my friends are mad at me for getting so frustrated about not selling any cookies. Maybe I got carried away. I just really wanted to win that trip to Pumpkin Paradise Park."

"Don't be hard on yourself, young Amelia," Wooo reassured her. "Sometimes creatures have disagreements, but these things don't last forever. It's a new night tomorrow, not to mention your *birthnight*! You'll wake up feeling right as rain! Keep that chin up."

"Thank you, Wooo." Amelia smiled. "You're right. A new night, a fresh start!"

Amelia tried to forget about the cookie competition and her friends for now. She decided to spend the rest of the night until sunrise reading *Positively Pumpkin* and finishing Squashy's outfit for her birthnight party. Feeling a little happier now that she had pumpkins on the brain, she stepped into her bedroom, straight into a puddle of goblin-slime superglue.

"Oops," Amelia squeaked. "Better not tell Mom about this . . ."

CHAPTER 8

THE PUMPKIN PATCH

"It's my birthnight, Squashy!" Amelia sang as the pumpkin alarm clock *squeeeee*ed at Sunday moonrise.

Squashy was bouncing around so much he pooped on the floor.

Amelia pulled on her best pumpkin outfit and dressed Squashy in the little bow tie and glasses she'd made for him.

"Mom! Dad!" Amelia called as she skipped down the spiral staircase. "Happy birthniiight to meeeeeee! Are you ready to go to the Pumpkin Patch?"

But there was no answer.

"Mooooooom! Daaaaaaad!" she yelled louder. Still no answer.

"Hmmm, they must be there already putting up the decorations," she said to Squashy. "Come on, let's go!"

Nocturnia was particularly cloudy that night. The only things illuminating the gray were the strange blue specks still floating across the sky.

"Come on, Squashy! Almost there!" said Amelia excitedly. "This is going to be the best birthnight party ev—"

Amelia stopped dead as the Pumpkin Patch came into view.

It was empty.

Not one creature was

there—not her best friends, not even her mom or dad. And there wasn't a single decoration in sight. Amelia stood in silence.

Maybe everyone will burst out from their hiding places and surprise me? Amelia thought.

THE PUMPKIN PATCH

She waited in anticipation. But minutes went by, and still there was no one. Did no one care? Maybe Florence and Grimaldi were still angry! MAYBE they had decided they didn't want to be friends with her anymore. The thought made Amelia's chin wobble.

Suddenly, Amelia heard a shuffle and a groan behind her, and a very green-looking Tangine limped toward her, followed by Pumpy. Behind him, a Mummy Maid was pushing a royal wheelbarrow full of cookie boxes.

"Happy birthnight, Amelia!" Tangine called. "Thought we might be able to sell some of our cookies at the party," he said, pointing to the wheelbarrow. "Karl is here to help too." The tall Mummy Maid waved awkwardly. Tangine looked as if he might collapse.

"Tangine!" said Amelia. "You're far too sick to be out of bed."

"I didn't want to miss your birthnight party."
He gave a strained smile. "ALSO, we need to
sell our cookies to win the competition," he
said, before frowning at the empty Pumpkin
Patch. "Am I early?"

Amelia sighed. "You're perfectly on time,
but it seems everybody else is late or has

forgotten about my party. . . ." She trailed off.

"Well, maybe if we wait a bit longer, they'll turn up." Tangine smiled. "Not everyone's as punctual as me!" He lifted a hand to pat Amelia's shoulder but ended up falling face-first into a pile of baby pumpkins instead.

CHAPTER 9

WHAT THE BATS IS GOING ON?

Hours passed, and still nobody showed up to Amelia's party. Squashy and Pumpy had munched through a box of Belly-Button Fluff cookies between them and were now trying to munch through the rest of the boxes in the wheelbarrow.

"No! I said you could have *one* box as a special treat," said Amelia, picking Squashy up. "You can't eat any more." She rubbed Squashy's tummy.

Ignoring Amelia, Squashy wiggled his stem impatiently and tried to bounce out of her arms to nibble at another box. "Hey, Squashy!

That's naughty. . . . Don't do that! I think you've had too much sugar!"

Tangine picked himself up from the ground. "I don't think anyone's coming to the party," he said, stating the obvious.

"Maybe we should go home," Amelia sighed. Squashy had started to bounce away into the cobbled streets of Nocturnia. "Squashy!" Amelia called. "Hey, Squashy! Don't bounce too far away, please. *Squashyyyyy!*" But he wasn't listening. Pumpy followed suit, the sounds of his PA-DOOFs fading into the distance.

"What's gotten into them?" Tangine asked, struggling to stand up straight. "Pumpy was behaving so well until now. Maybe Squashy has been a bad influence. . . ."

"No way!" Amelia argued. "Squashy is *usually* as good as gold." She grabbed the wheelbarrow and tipped it upside down so that all the cookie boxes fell out. "Quick, get in!" she said gesturing toward the empty wheelbarrow.

"Why?" asked Tangine.

"You're sick, and we need to move fast to catch up with our pet pumpkins. So get in, and I'll push!" Amelia said urgently.

Tangine scrambled into the wheelbarrow with Karl the Mummy Maid's help. Amelia tried with all her might to lift the wheelbarrow, but it didn't budge. "Yeesh, Tangine, you're heavy!"

"Hey! I'm a growing prince!" he said defensively.

"Argh! I can't lift it," said Amelia, growing impatient. She suddenly felt a tap on her shoulder.

Karl pointed at Amelia and then at the wheelbarrow. He pointed at himself and said, "Me . . . push you both?"

Amelia looked at Tangine, who just shrugged, so she climbed in. Karl tried flexing his biceps but decided to stop before an arm fell off.

Next thing they knew, Amelia and Tangine were whizzing along the streets of Nocturnia in the Royal Wheelbarrow. They passed the fairy exchange students giggling and munching on cookies. Amelia spotted a bunch of sparkly unicorn stickers stuck to their wings.

"I can't believe Frankie used unicorn stickers to get everyone to buy *her* cookies!" Amelia grumbled. One of the fairies caught Amelia's eye and screamed, then ran into the nearest shop.

Weird . . . , thought Amelia.

Farther along, Amelia and Tangine passed a post-bat staring at his sack of letters like he didn't know what to do with them.

"Whose letters are these?" he mumbled.

As the Royal Wheelbarrow turned a corner, Frankie, who was munching on a cookie, waved and called, "Hello, friends!" which Amelia thought was VERY odd indeed. She frowned. Frankie was never friendly to her!

But there was no sign of Squashy or Pumpy anywhere.

Suddenly, Grimaldi appeared from inside the Toad Top Hats store, wearing a top hat and holding a dustpan and brush.

"Grimaldi!" Amelia cried in relief.

"Karl! *Stop!"* Tangine demanded, and the Mummy Maid skidded to a halt.

"Oh, hello?" said Grimaldi, looking taken aback. He then tipped his hat.

"Grimaldi, there you are!" said Amelia. "You never met me yesternight to sell cookies for the competition, *and* you missed my birthnight party. . . . Are you angry with me?"

Grimaldi looked at Amelia blankly and blushed. "Um, I'm sorry, I didn't realize . . . I, um, I'm sorry. Remind me of your name? I'm quite forgetful." He looked at Tangine and waved shyly. "Hello, by the way. I'm Grimaldi Reaperton. I collect dead things."

Amelia felt like her stomach had been tied up in a big knot.

"It's me, *Amelia*. Grimaldi, do you not know who we are?" Amelia was unsure whether she wanted to hear his answer.

Grimaldi bit his lip. "I'm really sorry. . . . *Should* I?"

It wasn't often Amelia got scared. She used to fear unicorns before she found out that they didn't shoot laser rainbows from their bottoms, and she also used to be frightened of fairies before she found out that they didn't steal vampire fangs. However, right now, Amelia was *terrified*. Everybody around her—apart from Tangine, it seemed—was acting very strange.

She took a few deep breaths and tried to focus.

"Well, it was nice to meet you, Grimaldi." Her voice was shaking. "But I'm afraid we must go now. You didn't happen to see two pumpkins around here, by the way?"

"No, sorry. But it was lovely meeting you, Amelia. And *you-in-the-wheelbarrow*!" Grimaldi waved and floated away.

"*What the bats is going on?*" said Tangine in an unusually high voice. "Grimaldi didn't recognize his future KING!"

"I don't know," said Amelia, scanning the streets for Squashy and Pumpy. "But I don't like it. Maybe we should talk to your mom and dad?" Amelia didn't know what else to do, but getting help from the king and queen of Nocturnia seemed like the best thing she could think of right now. *Maybe they'll have the answers*, Amelia thought. *They ARE the rulers of Nocturnia, after all. . . .*

Karl the Mummy Maid wheeled Tangine

and Amelia back to Nocturnia Palace as fast as his scraggly legs could carry him. As they burst through the huge palace doors, King Vladimir appeared from the kitchen, munching on a plate of cookies.

"Oh, no!" Tangine cried, glancing at Amelia. "That was the emergency batch I left in the kitchen!"

"Isn't this exciting?" the king said to Amelia and Tangine. Then he suddenly looked confused. "Why are you both in a wheelbarrow?"

Tangine held out a limp hand. "We actually need to speak to you about that, Dad. But could you help me out of this thing first, please?"

"Of course!" The king lifted Tangine out of the wheelbarrow and eased him gently to a standing position. "You poor little boy," he said, touching Tangine's forehead. "I'm sure you'll feel better once you meet the *king,* though!"

Tangine frowned. "Um . . . *what*?" he said.

"The *king*! This is where he lives, right?" said King Vladimir. "I seem to have a set of keys for the palace, so he must think I'm super special!"

"Have you lost your mind, Dad?" said Tangine. "YOU are the king. Stop playing silly games now. I'm sick and need your affection."

King Vladimir put an arm around Tangine, who smiled with relief. "I'm flattered you think I'm the king," he whispered. "Just don't tell the *actual* king you said that!" He giggled and chomped on another cookie. "Cookie?" he offered through a mouthful. "They're really good."

"Um, Tangine," Amelia said through gritted

fangs. "Perhaps we should go somewhere private so we can talk."

Tangine nodded slowly as Amelia clambered out of the wheelbarrow and took his hand.

The two of them backed away toward the kitchen as King Vladimir sat himself on the front doorstep, eagerly awaiting the arrival of the king.

CHAPTER 10

SIT YOUR ROYAL BOTTOM DOWN

Amelia and Tangine sat in the palace kitchen feeling bamboozled. "I'm sorry your dad is acting strange too. More than strange. I don't know what's going on with everyone." Amelia put an arm around Tangine and gave him a gentle squeeze.

Tangine let out a groan. "I'm all confused, and one of my least favorite things is being confused. Why doesn't my dad know who he is?"

Suddenly, Queen Fairyweather popped her head around the door. When she saw Amelia

and Tangine, she gasped, "Sorry, wrong room!" and turned to leave.

"Mom!" Tangine shouted.

Queen Fairyweather appeared again.

"Oh, thank the grave! You remember you're my mom," said Tangine, clambering down from the kitchen stool.

"Sweetling," said Queen Fairyweather, embracing her son. "Of course. Now, where are the king and queen? The funny man on the doorstep said they live HERE. Come to think of it . . . how did YOU get in here?"

Tangine caught Amelia's eye and raised his eyebrows.

Queen Fairyweather scratched her head and flapped her glittery wings. "So, what day is it? Wait . . . I mean, night . . ." She appeared to be getting agitated. "Sweetling, we should get back to Glitteropolis!"

Tangine struggled to respond. "Aaah, I, aaaah, uuuh . . . ," he stammered, sounding like he had an orange stuck in his mouth.

"Tangine will be out soon." Amelia smiled, taking Tangine's hand. "Oh!" she said, looking past Queen Fairyweather. "I think I just saw the king and queen!"

Queen Fairyweather squealed with excitement and fluttered out of the room.

"Okay, something FREAKY is happening!" said Amelia trying to stay calm. But Tangine didn't speak.

He marched over to the kitchen counter,

grabbed a teaspoon and threw it out the window.

"Tangine," said Amelia gently. "I know you're worried about your mom and dad, but don't be a spoiled sprout."

"It's NOT fair." Tangine stomped. "We made ALL these tasty cookies that I can't even enjoy because I have stupid booger-poisoning, and now

nobody knows who I am. I AM PRINCE TANGINE LA FLOOFLE THE FIRST!" he yelled.

Amelia suddenly felt like somebody had dropped a brick in her stomach. "Wait!" she said, running over to Tangine and

placing both hands on his shoulders. "You've had *no cookies*!"

"Thanks for rubbing it in, Ameeeelia!" Tangine moaned.

"Well, I haven't had any, either, because of my sore fang! *Remember?*"

"Yes, of course I remember! We have both been deprived of our cookie rights!" Tangine was failing to calm down.

"PRINCE TANGINE LA FLOOFLE THE FIRST! SIT YOUR ROYAL BOTTOM DOWN

AND LISTEN TO ME FOR ONE SECOND, WILL YOU?!" Amelia yelled as loudly as she could.

Stunned, Tangine slumped to the floor silently.

"You have GOT to calm down," Amelia said, sitting down next to him. "Being angry and flustered isn't going to make things *any* better. It just makes you get all sweaty and slightly stinky. As I was saying . . . neither of us has eaten the cookies. Everybody else HAS. Neither of us seems to be losing our minds and forgetting everything, whereas everybody else IS!" Amelia bit her lip. "Perhaps, just *maybe*, it has something to do with the cookies?"

"What do you mean? How can the cookies cause this mess?" asked Tangine.

"I don't know—maybe there's something in the cookies that's making everyone a bit loopy," Amelia suggested. "Do you still have the recipe book from Mr. Sublime's cooking class?"

"It's on the kitchen counter," said Tangine. "Look, here."

Amelia flicked through the pages until she found the Sublime Cookie recipe.

"Okay, so the basic ingredients are one hundred and fifty grams of Sunflower Root, two spatulas of Powdered Scorpion Grass, forty-five grams of Rainbow Syrup, fifty grams of Leprechaun Elbow-Grease and a dash of Honey-Bee Essence. Then it says to add ingredients of your choice to personalize." Amelia studied the instructions.

"*We* added Raspberry and Fright Chocolate, Sweat Syrup Surprise and Belly-Button Fluff to our batches, which we *know* are fine because we've eaten all of those things before . . . so there must be something in the other ingredients that's affecting everyone."

"Maybe it's Frankie's cookies making everyone go weird," said Tangine.

Amelia considered this. "It can't be. . . . She added Armpit Sweat, Slug Slime and Beetle Brain to her cookies—nothing unusual there," she said. "So it must be one of the basic ingredients in the recipe book."

Tangine's eyes lit up. "*I know*. We could go and look in Loose Limbs Library in the north wing of the palace! We have every book imaginable in there! We're bound to find some answers," he said hopefully.

"Great idea, Tangine!" said Amelia. "We'll get to the bottom of all of this, I know it."

"I kind of wish we'd at least been able to taste *one* of the cookies," said Tangine sadly.

Amelia frowned. "Well, it's lucky we didn't. Those cookies are our main suspects right now."

"I never thought I'd see the night when a

cookie was a suspect," Tangine pondered. "Then again, I never thought I'd have a pumpkin with a six-pack! I miss Pumpy."

Amelia felt her heart swell for Squashy. She missed him so much too. "I hope they're both okay," she said sadly.

"We'll find them," said Tangine reassuringly. "And I'm sure Pumpy won't let anything or anyone get in their way, especially if it concerns food."

Amelia giggled. "Come on, let's go to Loose Limbs Library and solve this cookie mystery!"

CHAPTER 11

LOOSE LIMBS LIBRARY

Loose Limbs Library wasn't only the home to the king's vast collection of old leather-bound books about the Kingdom of the Dark and the Kingdom of the Light; it was also where old Mummy Maids came to retire once their limbs had completely fallen apart. Stray hands and feet shrouded in dirty cloth wandered around the stuffy library, in and out of the endless bookshelves.

The head of the library, Lawrence, attempted to keep things in order. He spent his nights gluing bandages and the odd discarded digit back onto hands or feet with goblin-slime superglue when needed. However, since Lawrence had no eyes and no body, most limbs ended up glued to various books, chairs and shelves.

"We need to look up every ingredient from the Sublime Cookie recipe," said Amelia, pointing at the recipe book. "I remember Mr. Sublime telling me that all the ingredients he uses are from the Fairy Forest, so let's look for any books on Fairy Forest plants."

Amelia and Tangine spent the next few hours trawling through book after book, wiping dripping globs of goblin-slime superglue off shelves and books as they went. Tangine had become rather engrossed in a very old and tiny book called *Fairy Family Trees*, while Amelia searched through the *Fairy Forest Encyclopedia*.

"Why are you reading that, Tangine?" said Amelia. "That won't help us."

"I thought it was about trees, but then I realized a fairy family tree isn't a type of plant," said Tangine. "Then I got distracted. Don't you think this looks a bit like Mr. Sublime?" Tangine pointed to a photo on one of the pages.

"We're supposed to be looking for suspicious ingredients," said Amelia. "Not fairy family history!"

"I know, but just have a quick look," urged Tangine. "This fairy guy called Ernest Sparkleton . . . Look!"

Amelia huffed and glanced over at the photograph. "It *does* look like Mr. Sublime, actually," she said. "Maybe he's related in some way. But come on, let's focus on the real aim of tonight."

"Wait . . . ," said Tangine, his nose stuck in the little book. "His son, Emilbus, is just like me—half fairy, half vampire!"

"Wait, what?" said Amelia. "How is that possible?"

"Looking at the Sparkleton family tree, it seems Ernest's wife was a vampire," said Tangine, studying the photos.

The Sparkleton Family

Ernest Sparkleton

Eliza Eclipsia

Married

Emilbus Sparkleton

"Why would they make that public?" asked Amelia. "Your dad kept you a secret for years! The Creatures of the Light and Dark were terrified of each other. . . ."

"I don't know," said Tangine. "Maybe the kingdoms used to be friends, once?"

"But that's impossible," said Amelia. "I don't understand."

"I can't believe there's someone else like me. I wish I'd known this Emilbus fellow." Tangine stroked the picture of the young vampire-fairy.

"Keep the book with you. We can think about this more once we've researched Fairy Forest ingredients," said Amelia. "Come on. Let's be as quick as we can—it's really hot and stuffy in here. And we've no time to lose!"

After some time, Amelia called out, "I think I've found one of the cookie ingredients in this *Fairy Forest Encyclopedia*!"

Tangine weaved through the scattered books, careful to avoid stray hands scuttling past, and settled down next to Amelia. She was pointing at a page titled *Sunflower Root*.

"Excellent, Amelia! That's definitely one of the ingredients!" said Tangine. "What does it say?"

Amelia cleared her throat, removed a mummified finger that was glued to the page and read:

"Sunflower Root, also known as Helianthus Root, *is a great source of vitamin M (which can also be obtained from moon-rays). It can be used as food crops for all Creatures of the Dark and Light; it can also improve the sight of vultures and be displayed as an ornamental plant."*

"Sounds like our vulture, John, could do with some of this!" said Tangine.

Amelia continued. *"Sunflower Root can be eaten in large amounts without any known side effects. In fact, it is said that three tablespoons of Sunflower Root a day can help one live a longer and happier life."* She paused and looked at Tangine. "It doesn't sound like Sunflower Root is our problem, does it?"

"Hmmm, you're right. There's nothing about memory loss there," said Tangine. "What else is in the book?"

Amelia flicked through the pages. "Ergh, I think Lawrence is sticking more fingers and toes to the inside of these library books than back onto the retired Mummy Maids!" She grimaced and peeled a firmly stuck eyeball off the page. "Maybe Lawrence could do with this eyeball?"

Tangine looked disgusted at the thought.

Amelia continued to flick through the pages and passed one titled *SCORPION GRASS*.

"Wait!" Tangine cried. "That's another basic ingredient from the Sublime Cookie recipe, isn't it?"

Amelia checked the *It's SUBLIME Time!* recipe book. "Yes, it is!" Then she read:

"Scorpion Grass can be found growing near rivers in the Fairy Forest. It thrives in the bright but damp habitat there. It is not to be consumed by living creatures due to its strong memory-erasing properties. If consumed, one's memories will transform into small blue petals, which will eventually settle in a suitable location and finally take the form of a forget-me-not flower, where the memories are stored until picked."

Amelia stopped reading.

"I think you've found our answer, Amelia!" Tangine exclaimed.

Suddenly feeling like she could faint from the discovery and the hot stuffiness of the room, Amelia wandered over in a daze to open the library window.

The room filled with a familiar sweet and flowery scent. As Amelia leaned out to breathe it in, she saw a couple of tiny blue specks drift past.

An idea came to her. Amelia turned around and pointed at the illustration of a forget-me-not in the encyclopedia. "Maybe those blue specks floating across the sky are actually petals—forget-me-not petals!"

Tangine looked at the illustration, then up at the window. "They're both blue, that's for sure . . . and they *do* look the same."

"Which means they could be memories!" Amelia cried. "Our friends' and family's memories. Look, it says right there: *'If consumed, one's memories will transform into small blue petals . . .'*"

"I think you might be right," Tangine said. "What else does the encyclopedia say about Scorpion Grass?"

"'*If the petals are then picked . . . ,*'" Amelia read, turning the page to read further—except there was no more. Just a new ingredient page about Daffodil Essence and a lot of globules of goblin-slime superglue.

"Hmm, there doesn't seem to be anything more about Scorpion Grass. . . . How odd. Maybe the page fell out or something?" Amelia pondered.

"I wonder why Mr. Sublime would put Scorpion Grass in his recipe," said Tangine.

"Maybe he doesn't realize what it does," said Amelia. "He said himself, the Fairy Forest is filled with millions of amazing and mysterious plants, so even *he* can't possibly know about every single one!"

"True," said Tangine. "Then we need to tell him right away! He might be able to work out a way to reverse the effects."

"Good idea," said Amelia. "Do you think we can get one of the Mummy Maids to find us a net so that we can catch some of the petals to show him too?"

"I'll get Karl on the case," said Tangine, nodding seriously.

"Great!" said Amelia, and she tucked the *Fairy Forest Encyclopedia* under her arm. "Come on. Let's go!"

CHAPTER 12

UNICOOOOOORN! THE TERROR!

Outside the palace, blue petals coated the sky like a flock of tiny bluebirds flying in formation. Amelia gasped at the sight and the intense flowery smell filling the air.

Holding the net Tangine had given her, she ran and jumped, trying to catch a small flurry of petals that floated above her head. But as she swept the net back and forth, it simply passed through the petals as if they weren't there at all.

"It's not working!" said Amelia.

"Let me try," said Tangine.

As if handling a large sword, Tangine poised

himself into a squatting position and grasped the handle of the net with both hands. His face was contorted with concentration and determination.

SWIIIIIIIIIPE!

But the same thing happened. The net passed through the petals as if they were merely figments of their imaginations.

"They're like little ghost petals," said Tangine. "What do we do?"

"We're going to have to hope Mr. Sublime believes what we have to tell him. Let's go and find him," said Amelia.

"But how? We don't know where he lives," said Tangine.

"Don't teachers just live at school? All the time?" said Amelia.

Tangine thought for a moment, then smiled. "Of course. Silly me!" he said. "To Catacomb Academy!"

The sight that greeted Amelia and Tangine as they left the palace grounds for the academy was not good at all.

Creatures of the Dark and Light were running around brandishing baguettes, top hats, branches and anything else that could be used as a weapon to wave, poke or prod each other.

Amelia and Tangine hid behind a gravestone as a Booger Bun narrowly missed Tangine's head. He heaved slightly at the sight of the boogers.

"What's going on here?" whispered Amelia.

"Get away from me, BEAST!" yelled a high-pitched voice. One of the fairy exchange students swept across the sky, and Amelia gasped as she saw Florence burst into view behind the fairy.

"I AM NOT A BEAST!" she bellowed. "I'M A RARE BREED OF YETI!"

Florence bumped into a young unicorn with a balloon. "GAAAAAAAAAAAH!" she yelled. "UNICOOOOOORN! THE TERROR!"

A crying cyclops rolled into view—behind him, an angel-kitten was trying to tickle his bottom with a duster.

Suddenly, Grimaldi went flying across the graveyard, screaming as a leprechaun jigged aggressively toward him,

yelling "Glitter
RULES!"

"WHO SAID
GLITTERRRRR?"
came Countess
Frivoleeta's shrill
voice. Amelia's mom
ran into the graveyard
holding two lit candelabras.
Her dress was tattered, her beehive
hairdo disheveled and her make-up
smudged. Amelia's dad, Count Drake,
trailed behind her with a pen and
crossword puzzle in hand,
looking a little
confused by it all.

Werewolves, goblins, skeletons and ghosts wailed. King Vladimir was running around shouting, "SOMEBODY FIND THE KING! HE MUST SAVE US FROM THESE HORRID CREATURES OF THE LIGHT!"

Then suddenly, out of the commotion, Squashy pa-doinged into view, blowing raspberries back at a pixie who was close on his tail.

"*Squashy!*" Amelia couldn't watch anymore. She stepped from behind the gravestone to rescue him.

"Stop!" Tangine shouted. "You can't go out there! You might get a Big-Toe Tart thrown in your face or something." Then he strained his eyes to get a better look at the crowd. "I wonder where Pumpy is?" he said with concern.

Tangine's mom, Queen Fairyweather, flew across the sky and landed on a gravestone that King Vladimir was cowering behind. She gazed at her husband, and for a split second Amelia hoped that Queen Fairyweather might still remember something. But then the fairy queen's expression changed. Her face filled with fear. She screamed and flew away into the Petrified Forest.

"Mom and Dad have gone crazy," whispered Tangine. "They've *all* gone crazy!"

"I think they've just *all* lost their memories," Amelia muttered. "The only thing they can remember is to be afraid of one another."

After everything they'd been through, the Kingdom of the Dark and the Kingdom of the Light were divided once again.

Amelia and Tangine stood in silence.

Amelia felt tears burn her eyes as she watched Squashy bounce away. "I can't lose Squashy!" she said to Tangine. "And I don't want my last memories of Florence and Grimaldi to be ones when we were fighting.

And my mom . . . she was so mad at me. What if we can't find the lost memories? It will be awful." Amelia's eyes filled to overflowing.

"It'll be okay. There's still time," said Tangine, putting his arms around Amelia. "We just need to find Mr. Sublime so we *can* save everyone's memories."

"I'm so glad you're here with me, Tangine," said Amelia. "Thank you."

"Don't thank me," said Tangine. "Thank the bad boogers. Otherwise I'd have been eating all those cookies too!"

Amelia giggled through her tears and hugged her friend tight.

"GAH . . . not too tight," said Tangine through a booger burp. "Don't want to throw up on your toes. That would make this night *much* worse."

Amelia and Tangine crept through Nocturnia, narrowly avoiding the wrath of confused creatures, until they reached Catacomb Academy. Amelia had half expected to see Frankie Steinberg standing there, arms folded and with a smug look on her face, having sold a bazillion cookies. Then everything would seem normal again. But the school was empty and eerie. Even eerier than usual, that was.

They entered the Coughing Classroom, where Mr. Sublime taught their new cooking lessons, but there was no sign of him. There was no sign that he had even been there at all.

The room gave a loud AHEM! Then sneezed. ACHOO! Amelia and Tangine ducked as a stream of snot sprayed toward them from the wall.

As they slowly stood up again, Amelia noticed that every decoration had been removed: the cupboards, which had once been full of ingredients, were now empty, and the walls were completely bare (except for the usual strands of snot trickling down them).

"Poor Mr. Sublime must've lost his memory and run away!" Tangine said, shaking his head. "Along with all the other teachers."

But Amelia was too distracted to agree—she saw a book on the front desk, picked it up and shook her head angrily. *The Truth and Terrors of the Creatures of the Light,*" she read out loud. "WHY are these horrid books still around?"

Amelia remembered reading the book a long time ago in a Creatures and Critters lesson, back when everyone in Nocturnia still believed Creatures of the Light were evil. But she now KNEW that these books were all made up. Every copy should have been destroyed after Amelia and her friends defeated the evil unicorn lords that had ruled over Glitteropolis and spread lies about the two kingdoms to keep them divided.

"There *is* no 'truth' in *The Truth and Terrors of the Creatures of the Light*," Amelia growled.

Tangine looked sad. "I don't think anyone can remember the truth anymore."

As Amelia and Tangine walked out of Catacomb Academy, Amelia tried not to feel hopeless, but she wasn't sure what to do next.

It felt like they had reached a dead end. And where was Mr. Sublime?

Amelia held the *Fairy Forest Encyclopedia* to her chest and took a deep breath. She looked up at the moon and suddenly noticed something about the blanket of blue petals drifting across the sky.

"Look! All the petals seem to be traveling in the same direction." Amelia quickly opened the encyclopedia to the Scorpion Grass page. *"If consumed, one's memories will transform into small blue petals, which will eventually settle in a suitable location and finally take the form of a forget-me-not flower, where the memories are stored until picked . . . ,"* she read out loud. "So maybe they're all floating somewhere to settle?" she said, feeling an ounce of hope. "They must be!"

Tangine nodded. "Then let's FOLLOW THOSE PETALS!"

CHAPTER 13

THE FIELD OF FORGET-ME-NOTS

The friends followed the trail of petals until they reached the Petrified Forest, which bordered the Kingdom of the Light.

Amelia felt a little lump in her throat as she looked back at Nocturnia and saw the Fang Mansion, her family home.

"I really hope we can fix this," she said with a sudden sense of overwhelming sadness. She couldn't imagine a life without Florence and Grimaldi, a life without Squashy or her mom and dad, or Wooo. The thought was almost unbearable.

Amelia and Tangine followed the petals through the Meadow of Loveliness, past the Wishing Well of Well Wishes and beyond. Finally, Amelia noticed that the blue petals were beginning to drift toward the ground.

As the petals fell, they curled and coiled, forming piles of small blue flowers.

"A field of forget-me-nots . . . ," Amelia murmured. The carpet of tiny blue flowers stretched as far as the eye could see.

Amelia stepped into the field and was instantly overcome with a wave of emotions.

Surrounded by the tiny flowers, Amelia reached out and touched one of the forget-me-nots gently. This time, rooted in the earth of the field, the forget-me-not petals felt very real. Amelia had an overwhelming urge to pick one.

She gently plucked a petal from one of the flowers, and suddenly the forget-me-not field around her faded and swirled, until she could see what seemed to be the inside of Grimaldi's barge.

Everything was a little misty, as if Amelia were in a dream. She saw Grimaldi, but he was tiny, no more than a few years old, and his grimpapa was handing him a present. She felt Grimaldi's love for his grandfather, and his excitement to be receiving a gift. Tiny Grimaldi floated around happily, tearing the black shimmery paper to reveal his very first scythe.

Then all of a sudden everything blurred again, and Amelia felt herself being pulled away. She was in the field of forget-me-nots, lying on the ground.

"Amelia, are you okay?" asked Tangine anxiously, leaning over her.

"I think I just saw one of Grimaldi's memories," she breathed. Then Amelia looked down at her hand as the petal that she had just picked disappeared. Somehow, inside herself, Amelia realized that the memory had returned to Grimaldi—and then she knew what they had to do.

Amelia sat up and looked across the field. "Maybe if we pick all the petals from the forget-me-nots, we can free *everyone's* memories!" She quickly picked another petal, and the scene changed around her.

Suddenly, Amelia saw an angel-kitten flying through Glitteropolis in the Kingdom of the

Light. Amelia could feel the angel-kitten's joy as the breeze whisked through his whiskers and fur. Then everything blurred and Amelia was back in the field of forget-me-nots. The petal in her hand faded away.

Tangine had also just picked a petal and was slumped on the ground. "I just saw a leprechaun's memory . . . ," he said, catching his breath. "There was so much jigging! He was in a national jigging competition. I think he won!" The petal in Tangine's hand slowly faded. "That was *awesome*! Let's pick more!"

Amelia bent down and picked another petal. The scene surrounding her changed again, and this time Amelia found herself in a dark room, the walls lined with stripy candy-cane-barred cages. She recognized it as the candy chambers in the Unicorn Horn Tower from which they had rescued Tangine's mom.

Locked behind the bars was a very familiar

large unicorn with a purple mane—Alpha Unicorn. Amelia felt his fear and saw a huge contraption being lowered from the ceiling. Manic laughter echoed through the chambers, and Amelia followed Alpha Unicorn's gaze to see a figure standing in the open doorway. A figure she knew very well.

A flash of light filled the room, and then everything faded.

Amelia felt an icy chill run down her spine before opening her eyes to see Tangine's concerned face.

"What's wrong, Amelia? You look so pale. Even for a vampire."

"I . . . I just saw Alpha Unicorn's memory," Amelia said quietly as the tiny blue petal she'd picked faded away.

"What? That power-crazy unicorn lord we met in Glitteropolis who tried to lock us up?" said Tangine with a bitter tone in his voice.

"Yes, and I saw someone else too," said Amelia, feeling her chest tighten. "There was someone laughing. But not in a nice way. And that someone looked just like Mr. Sublime. . . ."

"Really?" said Tangine. "What was he doing in Alpha Unicorn's memory?"

"I don't think Mr. Sublime exposed us to the memory-erasing ingredients by accident. I have a bad feeling about this, Tan—" Amelia paused suddenly, scratching her head and looking confused. "Er, Tan— Tang . . . *erine?*"

Tangine frowned. "Are you okay, Amy? I mean, Emma? I mean, Amelie . . . *What on bats?!*"

"I can't . . ." Amelia screwed her nose up. "I can't seem to remember your name."

"I can't remember YOUR name!" said Tangine, an air of panic in his voice.

"Tamborine? *Tin of beans?*" Amelia tried desperately.

"It's TIMMY BEAM!" yelled Tangine. "Wait . . . I can't remember my OWN name. I know I'm the future king of Nocturnia, but that's *all* I know."

"What's going on?" cried Amelia. *"What are our names?!"*

"TANGEEEEEENIUS!" Tangine cried. "I think my name is Tangenius. . . . That would make sense. Yes . . ." He scratched his head in deep thought.

"I don't understand. Why can't I remember—?" Amelia began. But before she could finish, someone who wasn't Tangine spoke from behind her.

"Clearly, you haven't done your research. . . ."

Amelia swung around and there, in the middle of the field of forget-me-nots, stood Mr. Sublime.

CHAPTER 14

PA-DOOF!

"Well, well, well, if it isn't Amelia Fang and Tangerine," said their culinary teacher.

"Wait. . . . That's my name?" said Tangine.

"*You!* You're behind all this!" Amelia pointed at Mr. Sublime. "Why did you trick us into putting memory-wiping ingredients in the cookies?"

"The real question is," began Mr. Sublime, "WHY haven't the cookies affected YOU?"

"A case of sore fangs and bad boogers!" said Tangine. "HA!"

"Ugh," Mr. Sublime said, looking disgusted. "Well, soon it won't matter either way. Soon, each and every creature's memory will be lost *forever*! I will divide the kingdoms for GOOD, and you will not ruin it this time!"

"'This time,'" Tangine muttered. "What does he mean, 'thi—'"

"OH!" Amelia cried, realizing what Alpha Unicorn's memory really meant. "Alpha Unicorn wasn't the mastermind behind dividing the two kingdoms for all those years and keeping everyone afraid of each other—YOU were!"

"I *was*, until YOU and your friends came along and ruined everything, *Amelia Fang*!" Mr. Sublime spat. "But I'm not going to let that happen again. I made a promise to divide the kingdoms for GOOD, and that's exactly what I'm going to do. . . ."

With that, he pulled a strange contraption from inside his cloak. It looked a bit like a child's bubble-blower, with a wide, shiny nozzle that was attached to a small glass ball filled with blue powder. It was a miniature version of the one Amelia had seen in Alpha Unicorn's memory.

Mr. Sublime grinned as he saw a look of recognition pass over Amelia's face.

"Yes—it's crushed Scorpion Grass, the ultimate memory eraser!" Mr. Sublime pulled a lever on the back of the device until it began to make a whirring sound. Then he paused and held up a finger on his other hand. "Wait. I almost forgot. . . ."

He lowered the memory eraser and erupted with manic laughter. *"MWAAAAAAAAAHAHAHA HAHAAAAAAAR!"* he boomed.

"Seriously? I've seen villains do evil laughs in the movies, but I didn't think it was a REAL THING," said Tangine, edging closer to Amelia.

"HAR . . . ahem . . . har . . . Oh HUSH!" Mr. Sublime hissed, looking at Tangine with annoyance. "I've been working on my evil laugh for YEARS, and you just SPOILED it."

Tangine gasped. "Did you just HUSH the future KING of Nocturnia?!"

"I'll hush, interrupt and interject whenever I please, tiny vampire."

"Actually, I'm HALF vampire, half fairy," said Tangine, flapping his wings and spraying glitter everywhere. Mr. Sublime stared at Tangine for a second, seemingly distracted, then shook his head and frowned.

"None of this matters now," Mr. Sublime declared with a dramatic swish of his cloak, pointing the glass ball of Scorpion Grass in Amelia and Tangine's direction. "I suggest we FORGET about the whole thing."

PA-DOOOOOOOF!

The ground shook.

A huge shadow loomed across the horizon. And then the biggest pumpkin you've ever seen (roughly as big as a small house) came bounding toward them.

PA-DOOF
PA-DOOF
PA-DOOF

"It's Pumpy!" Tangine and Amelia yelled in unison.

Mr. Sublime swung around just in time to see Pumpy launch himself into the air—and land straight on top of him with a big SPLODGE.

Pumpy then promptly fell asleep.

"Oh, Pumpy, how I've missed you!" Tangine hugged the huge snoring pumpkin. "How much have you eaten while you've been away?!"

Mr. Sublime groaned from underneath Pumpy.

"That'll teach you, Mr. Sublime!" said Amelia. "And now we're going to pick every petal and free everyone's memories. And *then* we're going to tell them what you did!"

"You'll never win . . . ," came a muffled but still-trying-to-sound-evil voice.

"We already have!" Tangine cried triumphantly.

Mr. Sublime wiggled his head and an arm free from under Pumpy's weight. "But you can't," he said, puffing and red-faced. He pointed to the book Amelia was holding. "It's all in there. . . ."

"What do you mean?" said Tangine. "We've read all about Scorpion Grass. We know it turns memories into flowers."

Amelia's eyes widened. "Wait, there did seem to be a page about Scorpion Grass missing. . . ." She opened the book to the Scorpion Grass section, but as she took a closer look, she noticed that the page in question looked thicker than the others, and there were purple smudges around the edges. Amelia gasped. "The pages are stuck together with goblin-slime superglue!" She tried to separate the two pages, but they wouldn't budge. "Aaaarrgh—Lawrence and his clumsy ways!" Amelia grumbled.

"Who's Lawrence?" asked Mr. Sublime.

"We need some glitter to unstick the pages!" said Amelia, ignoring him.

Tangine ran over to Amelia and flapped his wings as hard as he could, so that glitter went flying onto the sticky pages. Amelia rubbed the glitter along the edges, and finally the pages began to separate, revealing a whole other side dedicated to Scorpion Grass. Amelia read from where the previous page left off.

"If the petals are then picked, the memory is

freed. However, for every memory freed, the picker will lose a part of their own memory . . ." Amelia paused and gulped, before whispering, *". . . forever."*

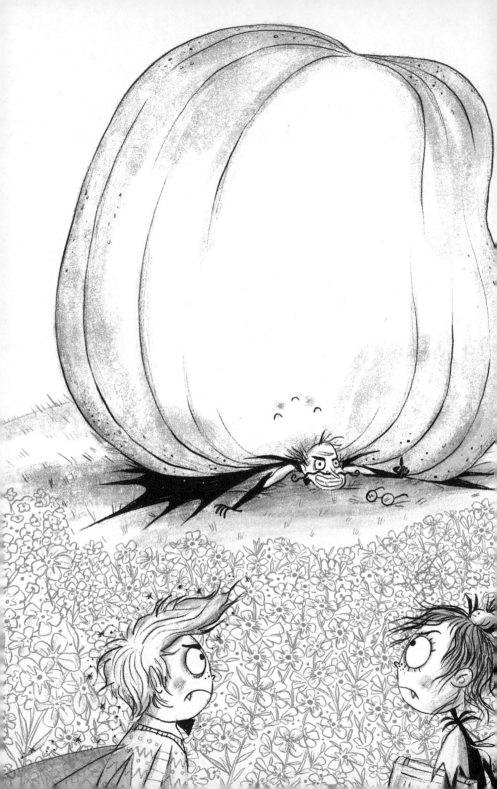

CHAPTER 15

JUST LIKE ME

"Didn't you wonder why you couldn't remember your name after picking some of the petals?" sneered Mr. Sublime.

"That's madness!" said Tangine.

"It's genius!" said Mr. Sublime. He let out another groan as Pumpy shifted in his sleep, then squeezed out a belated "Mwa ha . . . ha . . . ha!"

Amelia took a deep breath. "If it means my family and my friends get their memories back and the two kingdoms are friends again, then fine. I'm going to pick the petals."

"What?!" Mr. Sublime looked incredulous.

"But, Amelia, you won't remember your friends or family anymore . . . ," said Tangine. "You won't remember me!"

Amelia sighed. "I guess I won't know any different, and at least everybody I love will have *their* memories again."

Tangine bit his lip and then pointed at Mr. Sublime. "This is all YOUR fault!" He stomped his feet angrily.

CRACK!
ZZZZZAP!

A jet of blue liquid shot through the air, hitting Mr. Sublime right between the eyes. He squealed, then passed out.

"Oops . . . ," said Tangine, lifting his foot to reveal Mr. Sublime's memory eraser, which was now smashed into tiny pieces.

Small blue petals slowly emerged from the top of Mr. Sublime's head and danced in the air for a second, before swirling to the ground to form a bunch of forget-me-nots.

"You just erased his memories!" Amelia gasped.

Tangine looked at the forget-me-nots that had just formed and marched over to them. "And I'm going to STAMP on his memories to destroy them!"

"No, wait!" said Amelia, running to Tangine and holding his hand. "Don't do that—revenge doesn't solve anything. There must be a reason why he's the way he is."

Amelia reached for a petal from Mr. Sublime's forget-me-not.

"What are you doing?" asked Tangine frantically. "You'll lose—"

But Amelia had already picked it.

She saw an old fairy with glasses. She recognized him as Ernest Sparkleton from the fairy family tree Tangine had been studying earlier. Then a tall, beautiful vampireress walked in and kissed him on the cheek. She was holding a small child. "Ernest, my sparkling, our gorgeous little Emilbus just had his first glitter sneeze!" Then she stroked her son's cheek affectionately. "Still no sign of our little darkling's skin-piercingly beautiful fangs, though."

Ernest beamed and went to hug them both. "He's just *perfect*. He's going to grow up to do BIG things, I just know it!"

"Oh, yes, my dark one, let's give our little Emilbus whatever he wants, whenever he wants!" said his mother.

Picking more petals, Amelia became lost in
a whirl of memories. She watched the
bouncing baby Emilbus turn into a spoiled
little sprout of a toddler, and then a sulky
schoolboy who had so much that he didn't
know how to be nice or share with anyone.
When the other children came over, Emilbus
refused to play nicely. He pulled their wings,
stuck boogers in their fur and scribbled all
over their horns.

In the next memory, Emilbus's father looked worried. "Our son's wings are becoming less glittery every day," he said to his wife. "I fear he's losing his sparkle and becoming a real spoiled sprout."

Eventually Emilbus's classmates from both the Kingdom of the Light and the Kingdom of the Dark avoided him like the pus-pocket plague. Unbelievably, Amelia sensed a petulant Emilbus feeling outraged that no one wanted to remain his friend.

Emilbus stood looking out a window in his bedroom, flexing his wings. "If I can't make people be my friends, then I'll make sure NO ONE will be friends."

The scene changed. Emilbus, now a grown-up, stood at the same window, but his wings were no longer glittery. Any ounce of sparkle and compassion for others was gone from inside him. "I just have to choose which kingdom to begin with," Emilbus muttered thoughtfully, feeling in his mouth for fangs that still weren't there.

The memories began to whirl through Amelia's mind at the speed of moonlight—Emilbus standing in front of Alpha Unicorn and the unicorn council, passing around books full of lies and made-up stories of how dangerous Creatures of the Dark were; triumphant dances of glee from

Emilbus and the unicorn council as the two kingdoms became divided according to his plans. Finally Emilbus stood in a dark room, utterly outraged upon discovering that Amelia and her friends had defeated Alpha Unicorn and revealed the truth about the Creatures of the Light and Dark to both kingdoms.

Amelia's stomach dropped as she saw the grown-up Emilbus for who he truly was.

He stood in front of a mirror, wearing a smart outfit suitable for teaching, with a recipe book titled *It's SUBLIME Time!* tucked under his arm.

"Say hello to *Mr. Sublime*," he said, grinning.

CHAPTER 16

LOVE

"Are you okay?" said Tangine. "What did you see?"

Amelia shook her head. It felt light and fuzzy. At first she struggled to find the words. Then she said, "You were right. The two kingdoms *have* been friends before."

Tangine widened his eyes. "Wow . . . Mr. Sublime really messed things up."

"He did. But that's not all I saw."

"What else?" asked Tangine suspiciously.

"Mr. Sublime *is* Emilbus. He was a mean, selfish sprout from the very beginning."

Tangine looked at Amelia in horror. "The half vampire, half fairy I saw in this old book?" He pulled the little *Fairy Family Trees* book from his trouser pocket. "A boy just like I was—just like I am?" he said quietly.

"He is definitely not like you," said Amelia firmly. "You know that family and friendship are way more important than world domination. . . . Unfortunately for Mr. Sublime, or should I say, Emilbus . . . he can't see that."

"I *could* have turned out like him . . . ," said Tangine.

"But you haven't." Amelia smiled and put an arm around her friend. "You're awesome and kind and a bit weird sometimes, but that's you!" She giggled. Then she looked at the rest of the field full of forget-me-nots.

"I still don't think you should sacrifice all your memories," whispered Tangine.

"One person's memory lost to save thousands makes sense, don't you think?" said Amelia.

"But what if there isn't a way to get your memories back?" Tangine picked up the book and scanned the entry for Scorpion Grass again. "Look, there's more about picking the petals here . . . but there's a huge glob of goblin-slime superglue hiding it. . . ." Tangine shook his wings and covered the page in glitter. The slimy smudge dissolved slowly, revealing the following words:

The only possible remedy to restore the picker's memories is love. But the bond of love must be stronger than the loss of the memories.

Amelia felt her stomach drop. She remembered how mad her mom had been before this all happened, and how grumpy Florence had been with her too.

"What if when everyone gets their memories back, the first things they remember are the fights we had?" she said quietly. "Maybe they'll still be too annoyed at me for my memories to return."

"Don't be silly," Tangine said. But Amelia wasn't sure he sounded very convinced of his own words. "Just please let me help you?" he pleaded.

"No," said Amelia. "You need to remember everything so you can tell everyone what happened here. They need to know what Mr. Sublime has done so the Creatures of the Dark and Light never stop being friends again!" And before Tangine could say anything more, Amelia quickly picked a random petal.

The forget-me-not field and Tangine's face swirled before her as she fell into her first memory. This time, Amelia saw Squashy as a teeny-weeny munchkin nibbling on a maggot in the Pumpkin Patch. She could almost taste the maggot and felt her little pumpkin's joy before everything faded once again.

Amelia
looked at the
limp petal in
her hand as it
slowly disappeared,
and then she picked another.

She saw a young Florence on her first day of school, with glasses and a spotty dress, stomping up to a tiny Grimaldi. She felt Florence's nerves but also her longing for friendship with the little grim reaper.

"I THINK WE'D MAKE GREAT FRIENDS 'CAUSE I GIVE GOOD HUGS!" said the young Florence, in a still loud but slightly squeakier voice. Grimaldi smiled and the two friends walked hand in hand into Catacomb Academy.

Another petal gone.

Amelia opened her eyes and saw a young vampire-fairy with big white hair watching her. He looked worried, but Amelia couldn't remember who he was. She just knew she had to pick another petal, and another and another.

She saw a group of leprechauns at a party in a sunny valley with some gnomes; a monster girl holding the trophy for the Catacomb Academy's Most Spine-chilling Spelling Challenge; a jolly-looking vampire with a mustache putting his pen in the dishwasher, then later wondering where it had gone; and a stern skeleton teacher putting her head in a cupboard, accidentally locking it up and losing the key.

Another petal . . . Amelia saw a vampire king at the Wishing Well of Well Wishes marrying a beautiful fairy, then again at the same well, dressed as a ladybug before being turned into a bumblebee.

Amelia kept picking one petal after another. She was being flooded with memories, playing out like movies all at once. She could feel every emotion from excitement to fear, to love, to hate. But everything was becoming a blur. She saw blue petals all around her. She was picking them as fast as she could . . . but why was she picking them? Where was she? Why was she there? Who was the strange vampire-fairy watching her, looking so worried? Why was he worried?

Who was *she*?

And then there was just one petal left. She picked it with a POP.

Amelia saw a beautiful, noble-looking vampire lady with tall hair, standing with her hands on her hips. She was looking at a young vampire girl who seemed to have poured goblin-slime superglue everywhere. . . . The room was a mess, and a cute pumpkin was stuck to the young vampire's dress.

Then the scene cut to the noble-looking vampire lady sitting in a make-up parlour squirting some perfume behind her ears. Amelia could feel a mixture of emotions. She could smell the perfume. Amelia recognized the smell, but she didn't know why. She could feel the vampire lady's pride for her family, as well as her sadness for her daughter . . . and fear.

A regal-looking ghost wafted into the room where the vampire lady sat. "Your cup of Scream Tea, Countess Frivoleeta," said the ghost.

"Thank you, Wooo," said the vampire lady, before opening a drawer and pulling out a tiny black box with an orange ribbon wrapped around it. She opened the box and smiled sadly. Inside was a tiny fang. "My baby's first fang . . . ," whispered the countess. "Oh, Wooo, she's growing up so fast."

The scene faded and Amelia found herself sitting on the ground with watery eyes. She looked at the little vampire-fairy, who smiled at her and nodded.

Amelia felt herself fall backward. Then everything she'd ever known vanished from her mind.

CHAPTER 17

THE PUMPKINS AND THE GRUMPKINS

"Amelia?" said a voice.

She heard a **pa-doing** and then felt something licking her face.

Amelia awoke to find lots of eyes staring at her. Mostly because a Nocturnian multi-eyed monster was leaning two inches away from her face. Then Amelia noticed a bouncy pumpkin next to her. A huge fluffy yeti wearing glasses shoved the multi-eyed monster out of the way and took Amelia's hand.

"AMELIA," she said. "ARE YOU ALL RIGHT? TANGINE TOLD US EVERYTHING!"

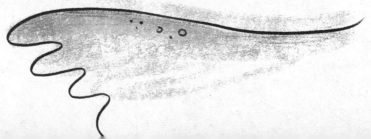

Amelia rubbed her head. It felt fuzzy. She was in a graveyard, surrounded by all sorts of creatures.

"I DON'T THINK SHE REMEMBERS ANYTHING . . . ," said the yeti, looking sad.

"Oh, Amelia, you're a hero!" said a little grim reaper with big eyes. "We're so sorry. We didn't realize the cookies were taking our memories away."

Amelia felt confused. Who were these creatures? Why did they keep calling her Amelia? *Maybe that is my name,* she thought.

A vampire with a huge frilly dress and very tall hair ran over. "Oh, Amelia, *darkling*!" She scooped Amelia up in her arms and hugged her tightly. Amelia breathed in a strong scent of something vaguely familiar.

Eau de Decay perfume. She remembered that was her mom's favorite.

She hugged the vampire lady back and took in another deep breath.

"Mom?" she whispered.

The countess gasped, as did everyone else. A goblin burped in shock.

"You . . . you know who I am?" said Countess Frivoleeta, placing her hands on her daughter's cheeks.

Amelia nodded. "I think so. . . ." She looked around at everyone else sadly. "That's all I remember, though."

The bouncy pumpkin pa-doinged into Amelia's lap and nuzzled into her tummy. Amelia giggled. "Oh, Squashy!"

"YEAH!" The yeti punched the ground in joy. "SHE'S REMEMBERING!"

Amelia looked at Squashy and her mom and suddenly felt so much love she thought she might explode.

But then she felt a sudden flutter of panic.

You're not mad at me?" Amelia asked anxiously, a memory of tiny handmade bow ties and ripped dresses slowing coming back to her.

"Of course not, my silly sausage-skin," said Countess Frivoleeta. "Darkling, just because I got mad at you doesn't make me love you any less. Oh, my dearest, I love you more and more every night that goes by. . . . I just want the best for you." The countess gently moved Amelia's hair out of her teary eyes. "And I know you'll grow up into the most fang-tastic vampire, whether you choose frills and party preparations or getting all . . . grubby in the Pumpkin Patch!"

Amelia hugged her mom tight. "I love you, Mom!"

"I love you too, my poisonous little pine cone," said the countess. "Oh, and by the way, you may have forgotten about cleaning your room, but that doesn't mean you can get away with not doing it." Her mother winked.

A vampire with a big mustache and a crossword puzzle in his hand wrapped his arms around Amelia. "My stinky little bead of sweat!" he said. "You saved us all!"

Amelia looked up into the vampire's eyes and felt even more love.

"Dad!" she said happily. "Oh, and by the way, you put your favorite pen in the dishwasher."

Count Drake chuckled. "Got it, my brilliant little bum-hair! It all came flooding back to me!" he said, pulling his best pen out from behind his ear.

"GROUP HUG!" yelled the yeti, beginning to squish Amelia and Count Drake in a huge embrace. She dragged the little reaper into the hug too.

"Florence!" the reaper squeaked. "I can't breathe!"

"YOU'RE DEATH. YOU DON'T NEED TO!" the yeti chuckled.

"Florence! Grimaldi!" cried Amelia. The feeling was almost overwhelming. She closed her eyes tight and hugged her friends back.

"TOOK YOU LONG ENOUGH!" said Florence, messing up Amelia's hair so enthusiastically that she fell over.

"This is amazing," said Grimaldi. "Your memory is coming back all on its own!"

"I'm sorry for making you grumpy," said Amelia sheepishly.

"WHADDYA MEAN?" Florence said.

"I got annoyed about not selling cookies, and about you and Grimaldi not wanting to bake . . . ," said Amelia, feeling the memories come pouring back and feeling terribly guilty about it all. "I'm sorry. I'd wanted to go to Pumpkin Paradise Park so much I forgot to make time for playing with my friends. *Are* we still friends?"

"OF COURSE WE ARE, SILLY BILLY! ANYWAYS, I COULD NEVER STAY GRUMPY WITH YOU, AMELIA. YOU'RE ONE OF MY BEST FRIENDS—AND I WAS QUITE ANNOYING, TO BE FAIR!" Florence chuckled and put an arm around Amelia's shoulders. "I KNOW HOW MUCH YOU LOVE PUMPKINS. AND I'D FORGOTTEN ALL ABOUT MY GRUMPS ANYWAYS . . . QUITE LITERALLY."

Amelia, Florence and Grimaldi giggled.

"A CLASSIC CASE OF THE PUMPKINS AND THE GRUMPKINS, I SAY!"

Amelia snorted and burst out laughing. Life would be so dull without Florence around.

A small vampire with fairy wings marched

up to the group with his hands on his hips. "Room for your *future king* in there?" Then he nose-dived into the huge hug-fest, sending a puff of glitter flying into the air.

"BLARG!" coughed Amelia. "Hey, Tangine, what's with all the glitter?"

"There you go," said Tangine, now draped over Florence's shoulder. "She remembers *me*. Surely that's *all* that matters?" Florence grabbed Tangine's head and pushed him off.

"YOU DON'T NEED TO REMEMBER HIM. TOOK HIM LONG ENOUGH TO REMEMBER HIS OWN NAME," said Florence to Amelia. "HE'S A BIT OF A TURNIP ANYWAYS." Then, in one arm, Florence scooped up Tangine, who blushed as red as a Beetroot Belch-Shake. "THE BEST TURNIP AROUND, THOUGH."

Amelia soon found herself being hugged by more and more creatures—King Vladimir, Queen Fairyweather, Sherryweather, Adonis the angel-kitten (who took it upon himself to dust everyone down with his collar duster), McSparkle the leprechaun, their teacher, Miss Inspine . . . and even Frankie Steinburg.

Amelia jumped with shock as she suddenly remembered the rivalry between her and Frankie.

Frankie stepped back and shrugged. "Don't get used to it. I'm still better than you in class," she said, folding her arms. "You should probably remember *that*."

Amelia looked at Florence and Grimaldi, who were holding in chuckles.

After many more hugs, a few eyeballs popping out and a bit of an issue with some goblin slime, Amelia came to realize that no matter what happened, her family and friends would never love her any less. Every high and every low only made their bonds stronger, and Amelia could feel that from the memories that were returning to her.

"Let me go!" a voice said, snapping Amelia out of her thoughts. She knew she remembered it from somewhere—and that she didn't like it one bit.

The crowd quietened and parted to reveal a handcuffed figure with thick glasses and a dramatic cloak. He looked familiar, but Amelia wasn't sure why. Two unicorn guards were standing on either side of him.

It was Emilbus.

CHAPTER 18

TAKE HIM AWAY!

"Did we give you permission to speak?" said one of the unicorn guards.

"Technically, we didn't tell him he couldn't speak, Ricky," said the unicorn guard wearing glasses.

"Well, Graham, he shouldn't be speaking— he's a criminal!" said the unicorn guard called Ricky.

"YOU MAY NOT REMEMBER," said Florence to Amelia. "BUT HE'S THE ONE RESPONSIBLE FOR ALL OF THIS. HE TRIED TO KEEP THE CREATURES OF THE DARK AND LIGHT AWAY FROM EACH OTHER. BUT YOU STOPPED HIM!" Then she added, "KINDA

SAD HIS REAL NAME DOESN'T SOUND LIKE 'SLIME,' THOUGH."

"I don't get it," spat Emilbus. "You freed everyone's memories, which means you were SUPPOSED to lose *your* memory for good. How are you remembering again?"

Tangine marched over to Mr. Sublime, holding up the *Fairy Forest Encyclopedia*. "It says right here: '*The only possible remedy to restore the picker's memories is love. But the bond of love must be stronger than the loss of the memories.*' So the effects are not completely irreversible. Seems you're not *quite* the Fairy Forest expert after all, Mr. NOT-SO-SUBLIME!"

Emilbus went purple with anger and made a strange growling noise. "I KNEW that! But nobody loves anyone THAT much! It's an impossible cure!" he spat.

"YOU WOULDN'T UNDERSTAND 'CAUSE YOU'RE TOO FULL OF HATE," Florence said. Then she blew a very wet yeti-style raspberry in his face.

"You could still be a wonderful person *like me*, you know," said Tangine puffing his chest out. "Us half-vamp, half-fairy fellows are a great example of how the Creatures of the Dark AND Light can live side by side."

"The two kingdoms will NEVER be friends again, as long as I have anything to do with it!" Emilbus yelled at him.

"Maybe some time to think in the candy chambers will help," suggested Tangine. "Mostly because you forget how fabulous I am. An unforgivable offense."

"TAKE HIM AWAY!" Florence bellowed. Then she turned to Amelia and giggled. "I'VE ALWAYS WANTED TO SAY THAT!"

"Sure thing!" Ricky said.

"Come on, you ol' crook!" said Graham, and the two unicorn guards dragged Emilbus away.

Feeling relieved that the last of her unhappy memories were now dealt with, Amelia had a sudden thought.

"Wait! Was it my birthnight?" She widened her eyes. "I seem to remember . . . nobody turned up to my party!"

Countess Frivoleeta gasped, and her left eyeball popped out. "Slivering serpents! It was!" she shrilled. "We'd ALL forgotten! Only because of those dreadful cookies, of course."

Amelia giggled. "It's okay, Mom. I understand."

"Well," said Count Drake, standing up and addressing the crowd, waving his crossword pen as he spoke. "We have so much to celebrate now, why don't we have the ultimate birthnight party in the Pumpkin Patch right away!"

CHAPTER 19

PUMPKIN-SHAPED DREAMS

Later that night, Amelia, Florence, Grimaldi and Tangine gathered in the Pumpkin Patch, munching on Iced Intestine Pops and Crusty Claws. Amelia was pleased that her sore fang was feeling much better.

"Booger, anyone?" said Tangine, walking over with a plateful.

"CAREFUL WITH THOSE," said Florence. "THEY MADE YOU SICK LAST TIME."

"They're just so good and juicy!" said Tangine, licking his lips. "Anyway, at least I didn't eat memory-erasing cookies!"

"SHAME," said Florence. "IF YOU'D HAD A

COOKIE, YOU'D FORGET ALL ABOUT THE MASSIVE WET-WORM I'M ABOUT TO GIVE YOU!" And with that, she slobbered all over her thumb and stuck it in Tangine's ear.

"*EEEEEWWWWWW!*" Tangine cried.

Squashy came bouncing along, wearing six bow ties. He pa-doinged into Amelia's arms and squeaked twice. *SQUEAK-SQUEAK!* PA-DUD-DUD-DUD-DUD-DUD.

Amelia, Florence and Grimaldi gasped as a HUGE Pumpy rolled into the Pumpkin Patch, squishing a toad on the way. He was no longer the muscly, well-defined pumpkin they had once known.

"Maybe you *are* feeding him too much, Tangine," said Grimaldi.

"I'm not!" said Tangine defensively. "I found out he ate the WHOLE palace's food supply when he and Squashy went missing."

King Vladimir waltzed over. "Amelia!" he said, beaming. "I have something for you. It's a gesture of thanks from, well, *everyone*!" And he handed her a golden envelope with a little pumpkin symbol on it.

Amelia stroked the silky envelope. The king smiled as her friends gathered around. "Go on, open it!"

Amelia carefully unsealed it, revealing four shiny orange pieces of paper inside.

"Tickets to Pumpkin Paradise Park!"

Amelia couldn't believe her eyes.

"Tangine told me how much you were hoping to go," the king explained. "So there's a ticket for you and each of your friends to spend a whole week there!"

"Th-thank you!" stuttered Amelia, feeling almost speechless. "But I don't really remember doing that much. . . ."

The king chuckled. "Well, hopefully that will all come back to you, Amelia Fang. But know for now that you and my son are the reason we're all standing here tonight. The reason two kingdoms can celebrate side by side."

"We totally are!" Tangine gave Amelia a friendly nudge.

Then Florence shouted, "GROUP HUG!" and everyone bundled into a huge furry, slimy, glittery heap.

After much celebrating and eating, Amelia and Squashy headed back to the Fang Mansion with her parents.

From her bedroom window, Amelia could see the whole of Nocturnia. The moon was full and bright, and post-bats flew across the night sky. She could hear Wooo drifting along the corridors, her dad humming while on the toilet (probably working on a crossword too) and her mom calling the count, wondering where he was.

Squashy bounced into Amelia's lap as she sat down for a while to enjoy the view. Even though her memory was still a little fuzzy, almost everything had come back to her, thanks to the love of her family and friends.

Amelia stroked Squashy's belly, which was full to the brim and gurgling with Gasping Gooseberries.

There was a light knock on Amelia's bedroom door, and the countess's beehive hair made an appearance. "Dare I look in here?" she said.

"Gaaah, I've not had a chance to clean up yet!" Amelia panicked, leaping up and almost stepping into a puddle of goblin-slime superglue.

Countess Frivoleeta laughed and stepped into the bedroom. "Darkling, I'm joking. I know I don't very often, but this is one of those rare occasions. It was a terrifically terrifying joke, don't you think?"

Amelia breathed a sigh of relief.

"Yes, *terrifying*," she said, raising her eyebrows.

"I wanted to give you something," said her mother. "Close your eyes. . . ."

Amelia heard some rummaging around and then felt something slide over her head and drop down by her chest.

"Open . . . ," said her mother softly.

When Amelia opened her eyes and looked down, she saw a little pumpkin necklace shimmering in the moonlight. Amelia gasped.

"It's wonderful!" she cried, throwing her arms around her mother's waist. "Thank you, Mom!"

"Well, you'll need something to remember me by while you're off traveling to all the different pumpkin patches as a world-class Pumpkinologist," the countess said with a smile.

Amelia couldn't quite believe what she was hearing. "You . . . you don't mind that I want to be a Pumpkinologist? I thought—" she began. But her mother placed a finger on Amelia's lips.

"Amelia Fang. You follow those pumpkin-shaped dreams of yours and do what makes YOU happy . . ." Then she added, "As soon as you complete your organ exams."

Amelia and her mom burst out laughing.

"Sure, Mom."

Amelia gave the countess one last squeeze before

reluctantly deciding she really *should* clean up. And then she realized something a little bit awkward.

"Um, Mom . . ."

"Yes, my horrid little leech?"

"I think I got goblin-slime superglue on me again," said Amelia. "I'm *pretty* sure we're stuck together. . . ."

The countess tried to move, but Amelia was right. The two of them were firmly stuck to each other.

"Well," said the countess, "I guess we'll just have to hug forever!"

"Doesn't sound like a bad idea," said Amelia, breathing in her mom's wonderfully rotten perfume. Then she looked up and grinned. "Does that mean I don't have to clean my room now?"

THE END

ABOUT THE AUTHOR

When she's not trying to take over the world or fighting sock-stealing monsters, Laura Ellen Anderson is a professional children's book author and illustrator, with an increasing addiction to coffee. She spends every waking hour creating and drawing, and would quite like to live on the moon when humans finally make it possible. Laura is the creator of *Evil Emperor Penguin* and the illustrator of *Witch Wars*, as well as many other children's books. Amelia Fang is her first series as an author-illustrator.